CHERILYN YAP

HELL EXPRESS
THE CAKELAND KINGDOM

ALL ABOARD! TWO BEST FRIENDS WIN THE ADVENTURE
OF A LIFETIME, BUT IT'S NOT THE LUXURY TRAIN
THEY THOUGHT IT WOULD BE.

Cover Design: Cherilyn Yap
Editor: Chrisandra Proofreads
ISBN: 978-629-97223-0-4 (paperback)
978-629-97223-1-1 (ebook)
First Edition: September 2022

CONTENTS

Dedication V

Corinne Lin 1

Claire Luna 2

1. Prologue 3

2. Chapter 1 7

3. Chapter 2 20

4. Chapter 3 30

5. Chapter 4 41

6. Chapter 5 50

7. Chapter 6 64

8. Chapter 7 73

9. Chapter 8 83

10. Chapter 9 92

11.	Chapter 10	100
12.	Chapter 11	112
13.	Chapter 12	119
14.	Chapter 13	130
15.	Chapter 14	142
16.	Chapter 15	153
17.	Chapter 16	164
18.	Chapter 17	179
19.	Chapter 18	193
20.	Chapter 19	205
21.	Chapter 20	216
22.	Chapter 21	226
23.	Epilogue	237
Acknowledgments		240
About Author		242

This book is dedicated to my ~~sanity,~~ I mean, my family, and my best friend for always believing in me.

NAME:

Corinne Lin

AGE: 20

SKILLS:

-Shaman-in-training
-Superstrength
-Sword master

OTHERS:

-Foodie
-Bubbly, optimistic
-Gets angry easily when hungry
-Childish, age 20 on ID card
but behave like a kid

NAME:
Claire Luna

AGE:
20

SKILLS:
-Voodoo doll master
-Observant
-Combat master

OTHERS:
-Bellina is her first doll companion
-Mom of the group
-Level-headed
-Have a group of doll companions

PROLOGUE

How would you feel if you got a free luxurious traveling package, but ended up in Hell?

Corinne wasn't even joking when she said *Hell*, it was literally printed on her train ticket—*Hell Express*.

When she got the train ticket from the store associate at Wilmart, the train ticket felt thick and expensive, it was a cream-colored paper with a swirly gold font. It looked lush and fancy.

But now, the ticket was transformed into something that looked like it came straight out of a horror movie. The paper turned black, and the curved font transformed into a creepy kind of text. Corinne wasn't sure if she was just imagining it or if it was real but holding the piece of paper gave her chills.

The thought of her being pranked popped into her mind and she started to wonder if there were hidden cameras around her just as the sound of radio static broke her train of thought.

Bzzz

"Welcome aboard Hell Express Six, fellow soon-to-be travellers! I'm your lovely conductor, Katie. I wonder how many of you are still alive after the little fiasco earlier.
I'm sure all of you are confused right now. Many questions are running through your mind.
Who am I?
Where am I?
What's going on?
Is this a prank?
First of all, no, this is not a prank and second of all, you are all on a train—Hell Express Six.
As a trial *traveller of Hell Travel Agency, I am not allowed to disclose much information. However, since I am a compassionate and kind person, I will use my authority to grant you guys one chance.*
Obtain the Traveller's Guide from our kitchen crew by ordering a suitable meal *from them.*
But be careful. Don't open the door to those who are not your kind. There are different species on the train, be cautious of who you welcome into your cabin.
Oopsie! I just gave out a survival tip. Oh, how kind and generous of me!
This announcement is brought to you by Hell Express Six of Hell

Travel Agency. Toodaloo, trial travellers!
Happy Survival!"

The message ended in another *bzzz* sound when the speaker was turned off.

Pushing all the confusion aside, Corinne had one thing on her mind and that was to get the Traveller's Guide.

To get it, she would need to order something from the kitchen crew.

She wondered what the train conductor meant when she said different species and what sort of meal was considered a suitable meal?

The sound of a trolley being pushed down the corridor caught her attention, but that was not all, Corinne sensed a familiar chill down her spine as the temperature dropped tremendously.

Knock
Knock
Knock
Knock

Corinne flinched when the knocking stopped at the fourth time.

Humans knock three times... Ghosts knock four times...

"What would you like to order? Today's special is the human thigh sashimi served with freshly squeezed brain juice."

Okay, now she knew what the train conductor meant by "different species."

CHAPTER 1

"Don't worry, I'll call you guys when we reach there," Corinne said, "plus, Claire is with me, if you're not confident with me, there's still Claire right?"

The Lin family stood on the platform of the train station. Corinne had her brown locks tied in a loose bun with a daisy hair tie, a bright smile spread across her small round face and her eyes beamed with excitement.

In comparison with the young brunette who was obviously in a good mood, her elderly grandparents were smiling as well, however their smiles seemed strained.

Concern painted both her grandparents' eyes, and Corinne felt odd about that. But she thought that they might just be worried about her.

She was already a twenty-year-old young adult, but she had never left her grandparents' side before. They were the ones who raised her, and she'd never known her parents. Grandpa George and Grandma Jane said that they died when she was just a baby.

She spent her whole life learning Taoist magic from her grandpa and martial arts from her grandma. This was the same with her childhood bestie, Claire. She called Claire's mother Aunt Amy, and Corinne learned about voodoo dolls from her.

They were strict with their teachings. Corinne remembered when they were young, she and Claire were tired from training and just wanted to play with their dolls. They threw a huge tantrum.

Corinne's grandparents disciplined her, and Aunt Amy had a mental breakdown. The three of them made it look like if they didn't take this seriously, it would be life or death.

"Yeah, don't worry, I'll be sure to take good care of this foodie," Claire said, jokingly.

Normally, the Lin grandparents and Aunt Amy would have laughed, but now they showed them those strained smiles.

Corinne and Claire exchanged a confused gaze, they both felt odd.

When a lavish-looking train stopped in front of them, Corinne grabbed her suitcase, and bid her family goodbye.

Aunt Amy suddenly ran a few steps towards the girls and pulled them into a tight hug. Tears welled in her eyes.

When she let go, her lips quivered, and she looked at them as though she had a million words to say, but in the end, she didn't say anything because if she would have opened her mouth, she was sure that she would burst out crying.

Aunt Amy knew that this day would come, she thought she was mentally prepared for her daughter to leave her and go to face those dangers. But now that the time had come, her emotions overwhelmed her.

She pulled Claire into a tight hug and suppressed her sobs.

Claire shot Corinne a worried gaze and saw that Corinne was giving her the same look as she was held in her grandparents' tight embrace.

Corinne returned her grandparents' hug and gently patted their backs. She could feel that they were trembling and the wetness of their tears on her shoulder.

When they let go, Grandma Jane grasped her hand tightly, "Corinne... please be careful."

Corinne nodded, "I will."

When Corinne stepped onto the train, Grandpa George and Grandma Jane came forward. Grandma's hands were outstretched as though she wanted to grab Corinne and pull her back to them.

"Please be safe and return home."

These words that her grandpa said kept ringing in her mind.

Suddenly, the train ticket in her hand became ten times heavier.

She couldn't get the odd feeling out from her mind. The looks on the faces of her grandparents' and Aunt Amy, all of them crying like they were...

"...Dead."

"What?" Corinne looked at her best friend.

"I'm talking about our family, they looked like we're off to die," Claire said with furrowed brows, "I'm worried about them."

Corinne couldn't agree more with her best friend.

Their families had been acting strange ever since Corinne and Claire came back with tickets to a free five-star luxury trip they won from Wilmart.

Back at the train station, Grandpa George stared at the departing train until it was out of sight. When he turned around, he saw Grandma Jane and Aunt Amy's despaired expressions.

"We all knew that both of them would eventually board Hell Express and become a traveller. We just need to trust them," the elder said, sighing.

We just need to trust them.

Grandpa George repeated this in his heart as if doing so could add some reassurance. After all, that was all they could do at this point.

They were travellers once and they managed to leave Hell Express.

However, the odd thing was that they had memories about all the danger they went through, but they couldn't remember how they escaped the train.

Just like both Corinne and Claire, their normal train tickets turned into a ticket to Hell Express, any train tickets can be changed, no matter if it was a bullet train ticket, the subway...

If you were chosen to become a traveller, no matter what, a ticket would be sent to you, just like how Corinne and Claire got free tickets from Wilmart.

The memories of the numerous dangers he went through came back into Grandpa George's mind; like how he was attacked by ghosts and monsters. Luckily for him, he was a shaman that practiced Taoist magic, so he had ways to defend himself.

Grandpa George didn't know why he was so sure, but he knew that one day Corinne would be selected by Hell Express. Which was why, ever since she was small, he and Corinne's grandmother taught her everything they knew.

That was also the reason why they packed some tools for her, so that Corinne could have a higher chance of surviving the danger that was to come and could battle those monsters.

Staring at the train that ran down the railway, Grandpa George could only hope for Corinne and Claire to be safe.

And to come back home one day.

Corinne and Claire walked down the train aisle; doors were lined up on both sides.

The whole place was quiet, the only sound that could be heard were their footsteps and the soft rumbling of their luggage wheels.

It was as if they were the only ones who boarded the train.

Their cabin was more spacious than what they expected.

It looked exactly like a hotel room. There were two single beds next to each other with a table and a lamp in the middle.

Opposite to their beds, a flat screen tv was hanging on the wall. A coffee table was placed in front of it along with a small couch, and on top of the table was a remote control.

In the corner of the room there was a door that led to the bathroom. There was a shower and a bathtub. Corinne took a quick glance into the bathroom and saw two sets of toiletries as well as a small basket of freshly picked rose petals.

What Corinne felt most satisfied with was the comfy bed; she felt like she could doze off any second just lying on this soft mattress.

"Corinne, what are you doing? Come and unpack your stuff," Claire said.

Ever since they got to their cabin, Corinne had been lying on the bed lazily.

When they saw their cabin, Corinne's eyes were beaming, and after that she laid on the bed, she had not moved a finger.

Corinne stirred, still with her eyes closed, but she gave Claire a wave. That was her signal for, "Okay, I'll do it later." Claire rolled her eyes and decided to unpack her own suitcase.

Corinne sat up and grabbed her cellphone from the bedside table.

She took some photos and selfies before departing, and she wanted to upload those to her social media. That was when she noticed that there were no wifi signals, mobile data wasn't working, and there were no bars either.

It stated that she was out of service area. Her brows furrowed at this.

"Omg!" Claire gasped.

"What's wrong?" Corinne asked, walking over to her best friend.

Claire was sitting on the floor with her suitcase open, but instead of the clothes she put in last night, it was filled with the voodoo dolls she made and some that were made by her mother.

The contents of her carry-on had been replaced by tools to make voodoo doll.

Seeing this, Corinne quickly unzipped her own suitcase.

Corinne felt speechless when she looked at the stacks of talisman papers, bottles of cinnabar powder, and brushes in her suitcase.

The girls exchanged a dumbstruck glance before Corinne spoke.

"I love how my grandparents think that I don't need a change of clothing or even underwear."

Even though Corinne said that, she still thought that her grandparents might be on to something when they packed all of these in.

Claire was thinking the same thing, especially with how their family reacted. Her eyes went over both her best friend's suitcase and her own.

"Don't you think they—I mean our families—had been acting strange ever since we came back from Wilmart with these tickets? The way they looked at us when we boarded the train and now this!"

Claire pointed to their baggage.

"…"

She ran a hand through her hair, all the thoughts in her mind made her feel slightly agitated.

Claire took a deep breath and pulled out her cellphone. She wanted to get to the bottom of this now. If not, she doubted that she could get a good sleep tonight.

"Chill, you're overthinking this," Corinne said.

Corinne grabbed Claire's cellphone, throwing it to the bed. Claire glared at Corinne, demanding an explanation.

"Maybe our families are just being overprotective. Remember how they refused to let us participate in any school field trips just because they wanted us to use the time for *training*," Corinne said.

"My mom did let me join mathletes and science fairs even if they required us to travel," Claire said.

Corinne rolled her eyes and went behind Claire, rubbing her shoulders to make her relax.

"That's not the point. Your mom was with you for the whole trip and this time it's just the two of us. No matter how old we are, we're always their little babies. So, they are just being overly protective and worried."

"Then, what about these?" Claire signaled to the voodoo dolls and talismans.

"Protection gear? Weapons? I mean, we don't have guns, so these are replacements. Relax, Claire. We're on a vacation! We should enjoy ourselves; we can think about all of those later.

Besides, you can't even call them. There're no bars," Corinne said, jumping back to the bed.

Looking at how happy-go-lucky Corinne acted, Claire let out a sigh. At this point, Corinne was swaying her head left and right, humming to her favorite tune.

"Fine, I'm going to the dining car to get something to eat," Claire said, heading to the door.

Corinne perked up, "Get me something!"

When Claire opened the door, she felt a gush of icy wind blow against her, which was when she noticed how dimly lit the hallway was. The lights were a dull orange, and they could barely light up the corridor.

Feeling bizarre, Claire gripped onto her cellphone tightly. When her eyes landed on the small voodoo doll, Bellina, that was used as a cellphone keychain, she felt at ease.

Bellina met Claire's eyes and blinked at her, giving Claire reassurance.

As soon as Claire was out the door, the door slammed shut with a loud bang.

The cloudy lights started to flicker as though they were about to go off any second and she could feel that it was getting chillier.

As soon as she stepped out from the cabin, she had been feeling cold. Was the air-conditioner supposed to be this strong in the train?

Bellina felt irritated by the sudden drop of temperature and she swung around agitatedly.

"Bellina, what's wrong?" Claire asked.

Bellina just looked at Claire and her whole body was quivering. That was when something clicked in Claire's mind: Bellina was not looking at her. She was looking behind her!

Bellina was Claire's first voodoo doll, and she knew her really well. Bellina wasn't shaking out of fear, she was twitching in excitement!

And there was only one thing that could make her this excited.

As the wind that had been blowing at her neck got stronger, Claire instantly ducked and rolled to the front, while Bellina swung forward, separating herself from the cellphone string.

When Claire glanced up after she got to a safe distance, her eyes widened at the sight in front of her.

Right on the ceiling was a ghost that was standing upside down, with her feet stuck on the ceiling. Her nails were exceptionally long, and her long hair was dangling down. When she saw Claire looking at her, she stretched a smile, revealing her vampire-like fangs.

The wind that Claire had been feeling all this time was from the ghost blowing on her neck.

Claire trembled only for a second because in the next minute, Bellina, who looked like a princess doll with her curly hair and puffy, frilly dress, transformed into a normal sized doll, and she lunged at the ghost.

The ghost sneered at the cute doll that pounced at her and stretched her long neck towards Bellina like a snake, her mouth opening wide as if she could swallow Bellina in one bite.

Bellina dodged and jumped onto the ghost's head, then she grabbed the ghost by the neck and slapped it against the wall at full strength. When the ghost got dizzy, she saw Bellina blinking at her innocently before Bellina's head became huge.

Before the ghost could process what happened, Bellina swallowed her. The ghost did not know how this could have happened, she was supposed to be the one who ate the doll and that human, but she ended up being eaten.

Bellina burped, tapping on her little tummy before she went back to Claire and jumped into Claire's arms like a toddler.

"Have I not told you not to simply eat things? What if that dirty ghost gave you a tummy ache?" Claire said with a smile.

Bellina pouted, staring at Claire as if she were asking her if she shouldn't eat the ghost, how could they get rid of it?

A smile spread across Claire's flawless features as she said, "Easy, we tear them into pieces."

Bellina's eyes twinkled as a similar smile curled up on her face.

"Claire, are you mad?"

Corinne's voice that should have been coming from the other side of the door, echoed through the entire hallway instead.

CHAPTER 2

When the door slammed shut, Corinne glanced up with a raised brow. What on earth? Is Claire mad at her because she asked her to get food while she was here laying around?

Corinne did not hear anything from the other side of the door, nor did she hear the noise from the battle between Bellina and the ghost. It was plain silence.

"Claire, are you mad?" Corinne went to the door, but when she turned the doorknob, it was locked.

Corinne kept on rattling the doorknob, but it wouldn't budge. She was stuck inside.

"Claire, I'm locked in!"

Corinne called out to her best friend while banging on the door.

Claire could hear everything and all the noises that Corinne made, but it was like she was stuck in another dimension with all the sounds coming from all over the place.

She couldn't find her cabin and the hallway kept leading her back to the same spot. The lights that lined the hallway continued to flicker as she ran down the aisle and returned back to the same place once more.

When Claire was contemplating what to do, the lights went out completely and she was immersed in a blanket of darkness.

The only thing that made her feel slightly at ease was that Bellina was still with her, but at the same time she was on edge because Bellina was feeling agitated again, and when she felt that way Claire knew that they were not alone.

A sharp wind sliced through the air, heading right towards her. Claire sidestepped, dodging whatever was coming her way.

Claire couldn't see anything without the lights, but she caught a glimpse of white as it zipped passed her. It looked like the hem of a long white dress that was identical to the one worn by the ghost that Bellina devoured earlier.

Bellina jumped down from Claire's arms and chased after the ghost.

"Bellina, wait!" Claire called after Bellina, but she was gone.

Claire wanted to run after Bellina, however, she couldn't make out which direction her princess voodoo doll had taken off to.

How she wished the lights were on.

As though her wishes were heard, all the lights came back.

Claire sucked in a deep breath as she felt like a lump just formed in her throat. She was engulfed in a wave of red, the lights *came* back, but they were not the same cloudy orange, instead they were blood red.

Huff

Accompanying the soft breathing sound were the lights flicking once more.

Huff

That was not a good sign, since she got attacked the last time the lights flickered and turned off afterwards.

Huff

She could hear the sound of the breathing getting stronger by the second; with the red lights flickering like this she could barely see anything.

When Claire thought that the lights would go out again, they stopped flickering. That was when Claire noticed it. A silhouette stood at the very end of the hallway.

Her face turned pale, and her mouth went dry. In a couple of seconds, the lights flickered again.

Huff... Whoosh...

When the lights turned back on, the silhouette seemed to have moved closer.

Before Claire could process what happened, the lights flickered once more. When that happened, Claire could feel her heart race and she felt cold all the way to her feet.

Huff... Whoosh...

Claire's hands balled into fists, and with her lips pursed, she began to move backwards. When the lights stopped flickering, Claire's movement came to a halt, and she felt she bumped into something.

Her whole body froze, and her breath got stuck in her throat as she quickly distanced herself from whatever she just bumped into.

"Claire, what are you doing just standing here?"

Hearing the familiar voice, she glanced over her shoulder and saw Corinne standing right behind her with her head tilted a little to the side, blinking at her with her big round eyes.

Seeing her best friend, Claire felt her body relax only a tiny bit. Claire swept her head to the other side; the silhouette was gone.

The lights seemed to go back to normal this time, covering the entire hallway in a cloudy orange. No silhouette, no lights flickering, everything seemed to turn back to how it was when Corinne stepped into the train aisle.

Claire felt relieved and the tension evaporated. Her cellphone slipped out from her relaxed fist, dropping to the ground with a light thud.

Bending over to pick up her phone, Claire answered.

"I was just—"

Claire's words got stuck in her throat, her whole body tensed up once more as her eyes went wide.

Huff... Whoosh...

The same soft breathing sound and the sound of something flew towards her.

Still bending, Claire flinched as her fingers tightened around her cellphone. She saw it.

Corinne closed the distance, and her feet came into view.

She was standing on tiptoe!

Claire couldn't stop staring at the tip-toed feet, who would walk and stand on tiptoe? Ghosts and spirits.

The *Corinne* who stood in front of her was obviously a ghost!

"What are you looking at?"

The ghost spoke in a voice that Claire was so familiar with and could recognize anywhere, but now all the ease she felt from seeing her best friend was gone.

All she felt was the chill that ran down her spine, as though a malicious snake was staring at her, watching her, preparing to attack.

Lifting her head slowly, Claire startled. *Corinne*'s face was so close to hers that she could see how ghastly pale her skin was.

Corinne was bending over just like Claire; her lips were curled up in such an eerie way that Claire was positive that this thing in front of her was definitely not her best friend.

Corinne's smile was bright and cheerful with little dimples on both side of her lips. Her smile was nothing like this ghost's.

The uneasiness and fear that welled up within her overwhelmed her so much that it was like tidal waves continuously hitting her, drowning her.

Glancing up at the ghost that wore an identical face to Corinne, the ghost looked at her with bulging eyes; Claire could have sworn that the ghost's eyes would fall off any second if she kept bulging her eyes like that.

The anxiety that reached the peak of what Claire could handle faded away just like the roaring waves that went still after a storm.

Claire's eyes narrowed as her eyes turned cold.

The ghost did not notice the sudden change within Claire. She tilted her head, wearing that wide, malicious smile.

"What are you doing? Get up and come with me."

A smile slowly spread across Claire's features, and she stood up, reaching over to the silver chain around her neck, revealing a bone needle hanging on the necklace.

When the ghost saw the bone needle, a sudden fear boiled in the pit of its stomach.

With a swift motion, the bone needle floated atop of Claire's palm, emitting a soft glow before a silvery white thread appeared out of nowhere and surrounded Claire.

"Why don't you come with me instead?" Claire said, looking at the ghost with a little smile on her face.

Claire loved how those supernatural beings looked when they realized that she was not some damsel in distress. Just because they lured her voodoo doll away, that didn't mean that she couldn't fight on her own.

The dim orange lights began to flicker slowly, turning red once more. Claire was seriously fed up with the light flickering trick, and she was even more frustrated with the ghost using Corinne's appearance.

With a flick of her hand, Claire sent her bone needle flying towards the lights. The thread was pulled along by the needle, a silvery white light zipped around the lights at the speed of lightning.

When it came back, a ball of smoky, dark energy was trapped in the white thread, just like a ball of yarn. Apparently, it was the ghost's black energy that was making the lights go crazy.

Claire tossed it up and down, her cat-like eyes glanced towards the ghost lazily as her lips curled up in a smirk.

"Now, it is your turn."

***

Corinne pouted, looking at her hands. Her skin had turned red because she had been banging on the door for five minutes and it wouldn't even budge.

She thought the doorknob might have been broken or something. Corinne also looked around the room to see if she could find anything that could tell her how she could contact the train staff.

When she could not find anything and her eyes landed on Claire's voodoo doll that was sitting in the suitcase, the idea of breaking down the door began to bubble in her mind.

Corinne went over, kneeling, and flashed her signature bright smile that showed her dimples to the dolls.

Apart from Bellina, which was Claire's princess voodoo doll, the rest of her dolls were mostly animals, if she didn't count that strawman.

The voodoo dolls that Claire made did not look like dolls that came out of a horror movie, they looked just like normal plushies with button eyes. If you didn't see how they were in action that is.

"Guys? Guys, think any one of you could help me break down that door?"

Corinne blinked at the plushies with her shiny, round eyes, looking at them with anticipation.

The animal plushies looked at Corinne before they huddled up in a circle as though they were discussing what to do.

Normally, only Claire would be able to make them do anything, but Corinne was merely asking for a small favor. However, the dolls remembered how Claire told them to ignore Corinne if what she asked for would cause trouble.

Is breaking down a door trouble?

The animal voodoo dolls don't have the intelligence to process this, all they could think of was to be loyal to Claire.

In the end, they turned to the strawman; while they huddled up, the strawman had crawled out from the suitcase with a beach chair and hopped to the table that was closest to the window.

Corinne followed the animal plushies' gaze to the strawman. What she saw made her jaw drop. Jax, the strawman, took out a pair of sunshades and was laying on the beach chair with a lollipop in his mouth.

Jax looked even more like he was on a vacation than her!

Corinne had no idea why he acted like he was bathing in the sun when she could see nothing but plain darkness through the window.

Honestly, the voodoo dolls Claire made always had such distinctive personalities.

Zimba, the lion plush who had a crown on his head, growled, calling for Jax's attention.

Jax barely moved from the beach chair and did a waving motion with his straw hand.

When Corinne was going to bribe Jax with her bag of candies, her cellphone rang.

Drinnnng

CHAPTER 3

Drinnnnng

Drinnnnng

Corinne's cellphone was vibrating and ringing on the bed. She went over and swiped to answer.

"Corinne."

Eyes lit up upon hearing the familiar voice, Corinne smiled wide.

"Claire! Where have you been? I'm locked in! I tried everything and the door won't budge, can you get the train staff to do something?"

"Corinne."

"What's wrong? Did you hear what I just said?"

"I'm here, open the door."

As soon as the sentence was finished, Corinne heard knocking on the door.

Knock
Knock
Knock
Knock

When Corinne heard that, she didn't move towards the door, instead she stepped closer to Claire's voodoo doll army.

"Corinne, what are you doing? I'm here, open the door for me..."

Corinne wasn't sure if she accidentally put her phone on speaker, but her screen showed that she was indeed on speaker.

She glanced at the screen of her cellphone and that was when her eyes went wide. Her phone screen was plain red; realization hit her.

Ever since she got on to the train, there was no signal, and Corinne had the habit of putting her phone on silent. The ringing sound was not her ringtone either.

So, who called her?

And how did she even answer the phone earlier?

She said, 'I'm here.' If it was Claire, shouldn't she have been saying, 'I'm back' instead?

Corinne felt like she must have been put in a trance.

"Why are you moving further to the back? Come over to the door and open it for me."

The hair on the back of Corinne's neck stood up as she shivered upon hearing what the voice said.

"...Jax, that..." Corinne gulped, "isn't Claire, right?"

Jax pulled down his sunshades and looked at Corinne with his button eyes. Corinne had the feeling that Jax just rolled his eyes on her and said, 'You think?' as though she was stating the obvious.

The animals were shaking their heads, telling her to not open the door. Corinne doubted that she could open it even if she tried, since the door was stuck shut.

Her eyes went back to the door, and she could clearly feel the pair of malicious eyes staring at her on the other side.

Since Corinne wasn't responding, the ghost outside became impatient.

"Open the door! Open the door! Open the door! Open the door!"

The ghost repeatedly said those words while it kept on knocking at the door as if it was trying to break it down.

With the ghost now screaming her head off at Corinne, Corinne placed her phone by Jax's side, stepping away from the table while covering her ears to save her eardrums from those high pitched, piercing screams.

Jax stirred on his beach chair, annoyed by the ghost's cries. He glanced down at the cellphone and tapped on it twice before he pulled out a tiny cloud of smoky energy.

His straw hands turned sharp and tore the dark energy into pieces, letting it vanish into thin air.

The ghost seemed to be shocked by the turn of events as she went silent for a second before she started to claw on the door.

Screech

Screeeech

The ghost was scratching and banging at the door, trying to tear it down. But no matter how hard it tried, the door still stood strong.

With how the ghost was practically attacking the door; this plain wooden door should have been broken down already.

Corinne suspected that they might need to abide some sort of rules, like they needed to get the permission from the owner of the room to enter. If not, the ghost wouldn't try to trick her into opening the door for her.

Grabbing a piece of lightning tempest talisman, Corinne was about to slip it over the door to give the ghost a piece of her mind when she heard a screeching scream slicing through the air.

After that, Claire's voice called out from the other side of the door.

"Corinne, it's me, Claire."

Corinne paused for a second, and went closer to the door, her eyes looking it over suspiciously.

"What's my favorite color?"

There was a brief silence at the other end before Claire answered.

"Rainbow. You like everything colorful."

"Okay. But anyone can guess that," Corinne said, rubbing her chin.

Corinne could hear a soft sigh and a series of impatient little knocks on the door, the knocking was probably by Bellina.

"When we were in tenth grade, you used me as an excuse saying that you were accompanying me to do my science fair project after school, but truth is, you snuck out to buy Prince what's-his-name stuff at some ComiCon."

"It's Prince Florian!" Corinne said.

Prince Florian was a fictional character from a visual novel game that Corinne was obsessed with.

Corinne was holding on to her lightning tempest talisman with one hand, while her other hand was on the doorknob. She glanced at Claire's voodoo dolls and seeing that they did not seem to oppose it, Corinne tried the door. Surprisingly, the door wasn't shut tight like how it was earlier.

When she saw Claire standing outside with Bellina, Corinne urged them to get in fast.

"Come in quick!" Corinne said.

Then, she took a quick scan of the hallway, but she did not see any ghosts outside. The entire corridor was dimly lit by foggy orange light, and she could only see darkness at each end of the hallway, it was like the darkness was going to devour her, pulling her into the deepest part of the abyss.

Corinne went into her room in a flash, closing the door and locking it.

When Claire stepped into their cabin, Jax was still laying on his beach chair. He briefly glanced at Claire and seeing that his master was doing just fine, he went back to chilling.

Bellina puffed up her cheeks and glared at Corinne as though she was unhappy because Corinne did not open the door immediately and that she had to wait outside.

Corinne flashed a wide smile and apologized to Bellina, giving the princess doll a bunch of candies. Bellina brightened up and skipped over to Jax showing him all the candies she got.

Claire's animal voodoo dolls all surrounded her jumping up and down, their eyes lit up upon seeing what Claire had in her hand.

That was when Corinne noticed two dolls that she had never seen before in Claire's hands. Both of them had horrified expressions glued on their faces. Claire used her bone needle and white thread to turn them into double dolls.

Double dolls are dolls that she could use when she faced danger, and the harm would be directed to the double doll.

"This one attacked me in the hallway, the other one was eaten by Bellina," Claire pointed to one of the ghost dolls and explained what she encountered after she exited their room.

After Claire finished with her side of the story, Corinne signalled to the other ghost doll.

"This is the one that stood outside the door when you came back earlier?" Corinne asked.

Claire nodded and Corinne told her everything from the door getting slammed shut to the ghost pretending to be Claire and calling her, as well as the part regarding the ghost trying to break the door down to no avail.

"Did our family expect this to happen, so that's why they packed our tools for us?" Claire asked.

"But how could they have known in advance that we would board a haunted train? And this is very odd, if this is a ghost train, how could I have not sensed it when the train arrived at the platform?" Corinne voiced out her confusion.

Corinne looked at Claire, her eyes went wide.

"How are we going to get off of the train?" Corinne asked, her voice laced with mild panic.

Corinne recalled what she saw earlier, a dark hallway and she couldn't see the end of the corridor at all. It was like they were trapped in another dimension.

Claire shook her head, brows furrowed.

Frustration welled up within Corinne as her mind raced with thoughts, her fingers subconsciously rubbing on her jade bead bracelet.

She had been wearing this bracelet ever since she was a little kid. Her grandpa said that it was something that was passed down in their family for generations. It had special protection runes engraved on the beads.

Corinne gave up on thinking any further, she felt like her head was going to explode if she continued to rack her brain on this.

Annoyed, she grabbed her pile of talismans, puffing up her cheeks.

"I will blow up this entire place if I have to!"

Bellina perked up when she heard this and came over to sit beside Corinne, nodding in agreement.

Claire squeezed Corinne's puffy cheek with one hand while squeezing Bellina's round cheek with the other.

"Don't act without thinking, you two."

Corinne pouted and turned to Bellina, throwing the talismans into the air, and letting them rain down like confetti.

"We're going to blow up this train!" Corinne said.

Bellina ran around the raining confetti, picking up the talismans and throwing them into the air just like Corinne.

Claire watched her childish best friend and her equally childish princess voodoo doll from the side of the cabin, feeling speechless.

Corinne was always so happy-go-lucky; she could be worried one second and calmed down by the next.

When Claire was contemplating what they should do next, a static radio noise cut in.

Bzzz

"Welcome aboard Hell Express Six, fellow soon-to-be travellers! I am your lovely conductor, Katie. I wonder how many of you are still alive after the little fiasco earlier."

Corinne assumed that the fiasco mentioned was about the incident with the ghost trying to enter their cabin and also about what Claire encountered in the hallway.

"I'm sure all of you are confused right now. Many questions are running through your mind.
Who am I?
Where am I?
What is going on?

Is this a prank?
First of all, no, this is not a prank and second of all, you are all on
a train—Hell Express Six.
As a trial *traveller of Hell Travel Agency, I am not allowed to*
disclose much information. However, since I am a compassionate
and kind person, I will use my authority to grant you guys one
chance.
Obtain the Traveller's Guide from our kitchen crew by ordering
a suitable meal *from them.*
But be careful. Don't open the door to those who are not your kind.
There are different species on the train, be cautious of who you
welcome into your cabin.
Oopsie! I just gave out a survival tip. Oh, how kind and generous
of me!
This announcement is brought to you by Hell Express Six of Hell
Travel Agency. Toodaloo, trial travellers!
Happy Survival!"

The message ended in another *bzzz* sound when the speaker was turned off.

Corinne and Claire exchanged a glance, both of them had only one thing in mind and that was to get the Traveller's Guide.

To get it, they would need to order something from the kitchen crew.

They both wondered what the train conductor meant when she said different species and what sort of meal considered as a suitable meal?

The sound of a trolley being pushed down the corridor caught her attention, but that was not all. Corinne sensed a familiar chill down her spine as the temperature dropped tremendously.

Knock
Knock
Knock
Knock

Corinne flinched when the knocking stopped at the fourth time.

Humans knock three times... Ghosts knock four times...

She learned this from her grandpa who was a shaman that practiced Taoist magic.

"May I take your order?"

Chapter 4

Hearing that question, Corinne and Claire exchanged a glance. Corinne gave Claire a nod before she pulled out a paper cutout. It was a plain, white piece of paper, cut into the shape of a human figure.

Corinne mumbled an incantation while she drew a spell in the air using her fingers. In mere seconds, the human figure paper cutout floated down to the ground and moved towards the door.

The dining crew outside knocked on the door once more, impatiently this time since he did not receive any responses from either of the girls.

"Excuse me, do you want to order something or not?"

"Yes, yes. Um..." Claire spoke, catching the staff's attention.

The paper figure slipped beneath the door. Corinne linked her senses with the paper cutout, so everything it saw, Corinne was able to see as well.

The staff was a skeleton. The skeleton was wearing a white shirt with a blazer over it, a red tie, and a black apron was tied around his waist with the words 'Hell Express Six' embroidered on it using gold thread.

A large silver dish with round lid was sitting on the trolley. His bony fingers were tapping on the handle of the cart, obviously losing his patience.

"What do you recommend?" Claire asked.

"The human brain meatballs and spaghetti tasted amazing, especially with the juicy brain juice that burst in your mouth when you..."

The skeleton seemed to brighten up, he opened up the round lid revealing said spaghetti that he so highly recommended.

Corinne, who saw the dish as if with her very own eyes through the paper cutout, instantly turned green, she covered her mouth feeling a rush through her throat.

She cut off her link with the paper figure immediately, and the paper figure slipped back through the door, lying on the floor lifelessly.

Corinne stormed towards the front door, tears welled up in her eyes threatening to flow down her cheeks any second, she covered her mouth with one hand while the other one was on the doorknob.

Right outside, the skeleton was admiring how the spaghetti was perfectly cooked and was confident that the humans will definitely let him gain entry when the door suddenly swung open.

He glanced up, a huge smile was about to curl up when it got stuck halfway. In the next second, his expression turned into a face of horror because Corinne bent over and...

"Blegh!"

The skeleton was petrified on the spot, his grip around the trolley handle tightened, his eyes were wide, staring at the pile of vomit on his newly bought pair of brand name leather shoes!

These were his new favorite shoes! He saved a month worth of his paycheck to buy them, and they were ruined by this human.

Anger boiled within him as he glared at Corinne.

Corinne looked up sheepishly, wiping her mouth as she smiled apologetically.

"You!" The skeleton growled.

Corinne could practically see the dark aura emitting from the skeleton.

An awkward laugh escaped from her lips as she took a huge step back into her room and slammed the door shut.

The skeleton must have been really mad because he kept banging on the door and shouting like crazy at Corinne for almost half an hour before he left.

Letting out a sigh of relief, Corinne smiled, "Thank god that he's gone now."

"Why would you do that?" Claire facepalmed.

Both Claire and Bellina were giving Corinne disapproving expressions while Jax looked at Corinne, speechless.

"I couldn't help it, I couldn't hold it in anymore," Corinne said.

After a couple of minutes, the same wheel rolling sound appeared by the hallway and screeched to a stop in front of their door.

The same type of question, but this time it was a woman.

"Do you want to order something?" Her voice sounded sweet.

Corinne was starving, she looked at Claire and said with a little pout, "I want a triple cheese deluxe pizza, spicy Korean fried chicken, double fish patty burger with extra cheese, large fries..."

Before Corinne could list out her three pages long order of food, Claire thought for a moment before she said, "I can't decide, what do you normally like to eat?"

"You can try Today's Special. The chef made eyeball soup and human thigh sashimi."

"Next!" Corinne cried.

After who knows how many times of the same thing, Corinne was losing her patience, so was Bellina; she was still a little doll, she needed to eat on time!

When the next dining crew came, Corinne held onto her talismans while Bellina stood beside her, balling up her tiny fists.

Claire wanted to say the usual stuff to test them, but Corinne punched at the door and yelled.

"Don't try to trick me again with your spicy human brain, eyeball soup or whatever! I've had it! I have a storm of lightning strikes and I'm not afraid to use them! And I'm going to complain about you to the travel agency for not serving something edible and letting your customers starve!" Corinne finally burst because she was starving.

"Well?" after Corinne's outburst, she was panting.

"..."

There was a brief silence before whoever was on the other side of the door answered. Claire swore that the staff's voice was shaky.

"We got triple cheese deluxe pizza, spicy Korean fried chicken, double fish patty burger with extra cheese, large fries..."

Claire was stunned when the staff literally repeated the same order that Corinne said the earlier.

Corinne crossed her arms, nodding in satisfaction, "We also want dessert for our little princess!"

"O-of course, Ma'am."

Corinne reached for the doorknob, "Don't try anything funny, I'm not joking about giving you a lightning strike."

Before she opened the door, she thought for a second and decided to send the white, human figure, paper cut-out through the door once more.

Linking her senses with the paper figure, at first, she thought she finally saw a living human being until she saw the death spots on the guy's skin.

It was a walking corpse. He wore the same uniform as the skeleton she saw the first time, but instead of the blank apron, this guy's apron was white.

The only thing in front of him was the same silver dish with round lid, Corinne wondered how he was going to provide the food she ordered.

She saw the corpse open the round lid, revealing a bowl of eyeball soup. This time, Corinne managed to prevent herself from throwing up.

The guy let out a 'tck' seeing that the dish wasn't the one he needed, so he closed the lid and tapped on it a couple of times before he opened it again.

This time the eyeball soup was gone, and a slice of pizza appeared of the silver plate.

So, this was how they did it. The food they offered really depended on the dining crew themselves, they served whatever they wanted by tapping on the round lid and made food appear on the plate.

Corinne cut off her link with the paper figure and the paper figure slipped back to their room, returning to Corinne's hand.

In the end, Corinne only opened a little gap and a pale hand slid in holding a huge plastic bag of packed food.

"Thank you," Corinne immediately took the food from the walking corpse and went to the table with the excited Bellina to enjoy their lunch.

Claire, however, was more concerned about the traveller's guide. Since the train conductor mentioned that if they ordered a *suitable meal*, they should be getting the guide at the same time.

She was going to ask the corpse about it when she spotted a 'thank you' card on the ground, it must have slipped out from the plastic bag.

Picking it up, she saw it had, *'Thank you for ordering from me,'* printed in pastel colored bubble font. At the bottom of it said, *'Please leave a five-star review for me, signed Larrie Mac Jr.'*

When Claire was going to toss the card to the side, she spotted a tiny QR code printed on the back of the card. Beside the QR code, she saw a Hell Travel Agency logo printed on it.

Claire only hesitated for a second before she scanned the QR code, and an app was downloaded to her cellphone. She had no idea how Hell Travel Agency did it, but the app was successfully downloaded even though her phone still showed no signal.

When she tapped on the app, a message popped out right away.

It said, *'Congratulations on your success in locating the Hell Express app! This will serve as a guide to answer many of your questions.'*

Claire internally cursed the travel agency and the train; they were so cunning. If she didn't spot the extra tiny QR code, she would've missed it. This app was the *Traveller's Guide*.

"Corinne, come and download this," Claire said, wanting to walk over to her best friend when she felt a pull on the hem of her top.

Glancing down, it was the hand of that walking corpse.

"Um... you guys need to pay for the food," the corpse said.

The corpse had been waiting for quite some time outside, he was afraid that the girl would strike him with lightning if he made her mad. Realizing that they had forgotten about him, he mustered up the courage to ask for payment.

"Uh... right, how do I pay you?" Claire asked.

She had no idea what currency they took. Was it some sort of ghost money? Did they even take human cash?

"Here, my grandpa packed some joss papers for me," Corinne said, stuffing a stack of joss papers for the guy.

The corpse paused, then, through the small gap of the door, he stared at Corinne bitterly.

"What?" Corinne tilted her head, then she glanced at Claire, "guess they don't take joss papers as payment then."

Claire rolled her eyes, "You think…"

The corpse retracted his hand back and after a brief second, he came back with a QR code. He used his other free hand to point at their phones, "We only take traveller points (tp)."

After Claire called out to her earlier, Corinne already downloaded the Hell Express app.

She hadn't navigated through it yet; she glanced at the screen and saw an icon that looked like a wallet. She tapped on it and scanned the QR code.

The corpse seemed very satisfied after he received payment. He mustered up a really sweet voice that left the two girls in goosebumps.

"Thank you for ordering from me, enjoy your meal."

CHAPTER 5

A registration page popped up when Corinne tried to navigate through the Hell Express app.

Please enter your traveller name.

Corinne tapped on the screen.

Sailor Moon.

-Name has been taken.

Superman.

-Name has been taken, you may try Superman12345.

"..."

Corinne stole a glance at Claire and saw that she had the same identical expression as her; she must be going through the same thing.

Cutie Pie Princess.

-Name has been taken.

'Are you kidding me?' Corinne thought.

Fudge You Traveller Name.

-Please refrain from using profanity words. Warning #1.

"..."

King of The World.

-Registration Successful.

"Corinne, what name did you use?" Claire asked, "I'm Doll Queen1113."

"...King of The World," Corinne said, eyes twitching.

Luckily, nobody will know that that was her name, it was so embarrassing. It was definitely better than Cutie Pie Princess... right?

The app was fairly simple.

There were a couple of functions: Profile, Shop, Forum, Customer Service, and Wallet.

Both the 'Profile' and 'Shop' icons were grey, whereas the other icons looked normal.

The reason they downloaded this app was to find out more about Hell Travel Agency and Hell Express.

So, Corinne instantly clicked 'Forum.'

There were a couple of posts that were pinned on top. Corinne clicked on the post that said, 'Newbie Traveller's Guide: All You Need to Know + FAQ.' and started to read through it.

I'm Superman012, I wrote this post to clear the confusion of newbie travellers.

I will cover some of the basics and if you want to know more about Hell Express, you can dive deeper into the forum, there are many travellers here who are willing to share their experiences.

Everyone who boarded Hell Express will be called 'Traveller.' After you finish registering your profile in the app, you will get a passport.

Nobody knows how one is selected to become a traveller, maybe it is random, and nobody knows how to leave the train and go home.

There is only one thing we need to do here and that is to survive!

All travellers will have to go through stations. Once your next station is confirmed, when the time comes, you'll be teleported to the station. Be prepared ahead of time.

You all must have played games before, right? Basically, Station = Dungeon.

There are two main types of stations, Wit and Slay.

Wit: Mysteries, puzzles.

Wit type stations require you to search for clues to piece the puzzles together in order to solve some sort of mystery.

Slay: Kill monsters.

For this one, you use more brawn than brains. You'll need to kill your way through the slay stations. It may be monsters, zombies, ghosts, spirits; anything that tries to kill you, you kill them first.

Don't take this lightly, there are no save and load, no bonus lives, if you die in a station, you are dead for good!

There is also another way to leave that station. You will need to find the 'Return Stamp.'

The Return Stamp is basically like a ticket to go back to your train. Once you find it, you just need to stamp it on your passport.

But bear in mind that using the stamp to leave will lead you to earn only a bare minimum of points and points are crucial.

Points are the currency among travellers and trains. It is important because you need points to buy food and different things in the shop.

The shop is just like the shop when you play games. You can buy weapons, skills, potions, and things of that nature. You can also pay a rental fee to open your own shop.

You earn points by completing missions at each station.

The higher the rank of performance upon completion of missions, the higher the points you get.

You can also earn points by getting titles, titles are gained based on your performance at a station.

This post definitely shed some light into the situation for Corinne and Claire.

If there was a Return Stamp, Corinne wondered if there was a Home Stamp, one where you can return home.

Seeing the two grey icons, Corinne tried to tap on 'Profile' and...

Access Denied.

She tapped on 'Shop.'

Access Denied.

"..."

Corinne looked up from her phone screen and saw that Claire was still looking at the forum, probably reading some other posts.

Knock
Knock
Knock
Knock

"Hell Post! Delivery for King of the World and Doll Queen 1113!"

Bellina went to get the door and came back with two brown envelopes.

Within the envelopes were the passports that were mentioned in the forum post.

They had red covers with 'Hell Travel Agency' printed on them in golden font. Corinne saw her photo ID on the first page along with her name.

It said:
Traveller Name: King of The World
Hell Express: Six

Bzzz

The same static sound appeared before an announcement.

"Attention all Hell Express Six travellers, we will be stopping at Cakeland Kingdom tomorrow at 10AM, breakfast will be served starting from 8AM.

To ensure all travellers are on time to leave the train, lights will be out at 9PM.

It is compulsory for all travellers to be on schedule at all destinations in order to avoid any inconveniences between all parties. On a side note, to celebrate the opening of Hell Express Six, Hell Travel Agency will be providing a welcome package for our new

travellers.
Have a good night and be safe."

The announcement ended in an eerie tone.

'Be safe?' Corinne's gut feeling was telling her that something would happen at night. With how evil the train and the travel agency were, Corinne doubted that they would let them have a *good* night.

"Corinne, look!" Claire said, pointing to the passport.

A new page had magically appeared in their passports.

It said:

Station: Cakeland Kingdom

Time: 10AM

Knock

Knock

Knock

Knock

"Hell Post! Package for King of the World and Doll Queen 1113!"

Claire went over to the door with Bellina on her shoulder just to be safe. It should have been the welcome package from the travel agency.

"What is it?" Corinne asked.

The announcer said that it was a welcome package, but Claire came back holding two white envelopes.

"Lucky Draw Coupon?" Claire looked at the piece of paper in the envelope.

There was a QR code for them to scan on the coupon.

When Corinne scanned it, a lucky draw wheel appeared on the screen.

There were different items on it: a toothpick, a lock of hair, sunshades, key ring, etc.

The wheel started to spin and then it stopped.

Better luck next time!

"..."

Corinne had reason to believe that Hell Travel Agency had something against her.

"What did you get? It says here that I got a potato lightbulb," Claire said, showing her cellphone screen to Corinne.

Corinne pouted and showed Claire her screen, "I got nothing."

She felt disappointed, but at the same time she was happy for Claire because she got something from the lucky draw.

Claire silently patted Corinne on the head, comforting her.

When Claire's package came, they exchanged a glance, staring at the item in front of them.

It was literally a potato with a lightbulb sticking on it.

The lightbulb came with a card stating the function of the item.

[Potato Lightbulb Experiment Invention 008 (made by Scientist Alfred, distributed by Hell Travel Agency) Protective barrier. Can be used as a shield or as a light source.

Barrier activation count: 3

Due to this being an experimental item, the functionality is not guaranteed, maybe it can be used as an ordinary lightbulb?

Barrier functionality not guaranteed, Scientist Alfred and Hell Travel Agency will not be responsible for any consequences.

Life is precious, use it at your own risk.]

'Such a fraud!' Corinne's eyes twitched after reading the card in Claire's hand.

Even the items they provide are defective! Shitty travel agency.

When Claire finished reading the description on the card, she already treated it as an ordinary lightbulb.

Just imagine what could happen if a ghost dashed forward, attacking you, and you whipped out this potato lightbulb. It lit up, but the barrier didn't appear.

Corinne waved the potato lightbulb at Claire, "This is a flawed item, it's better to make our own weapons than rely on this."

Claire nodded; her eyes went over to the wall clock.

"We better get ready for bed, don't forget, lights out at 9pm."

Dong

Dong

Dong

.

.

.

When the clock struck nine, the lights went out instantly.

The entire train went silent for a time, and then the sound of high heels clicking on the floor came from the other end of the hallway and it grew louder as it approached Corinne and Claire's cabin.

"It's 9pm! It's 9pm! Time to make rounds to see who is not asleep! Who is the naughty one?" The train crew member who was making rounds said in a sing-song voice as she skipped down the hallway.

"Teehee! Someone is not sleeping; I can sense it. Someone is not sleeping!"

The train crew member slowly opened the door, went in, and then…

And then…

She froze.

Inside the room, she saw a brunette lying flat on her stomach on the bed, her legs were swinging back and forth as she was engrossed in her cellphone.

Hearing the door being opened, she glanced up and their eyes locked.

The brunette was Corinne, she couldn't sleep, so she was playing games using her cellphone.

The entire room was dark, the only light came from Corinne's cellphone. Seeing a stranger standing by the door, Corinne's eyes did not move away from that intruder, her hand went over to the table lamp to turn it on.

Corinne raised a brow; her eyes went down to the name tag on the train crew member's uniform.

"Maddie?"

Under the dim lighting, Corinne could see that Maddie was just like the dining crew member from earlier in the day, a walking corpse.

Corinne recalled the announcement from the train conductor earlier about lights out at 9PM, how she wished them to have a good night and be safe.

With the way those beings from the travel agency and the train had been acting ever since she got on the train, she knew they wouldn't let them have it easy.

Maddie blinked, surprised to see someone being so calm when they faced her.

Corinne put up a finger and pointed to Claire who was sleeping on the other bed.

"Shhhh, she is sleeping." Corinne said with a smile.

Maddie blinked a couple more times as if her brain were stuck on loading.

Then, she took a step forward, planning to pounce at Corinne.

"I wouldn't do that if I were you," Corinne said, pointing to the floor.

Maddie glanced down and that was when she saw it, Corinne's bed was surrounded by her lightning tempest talismans.

Corinne's lips curled up as she put down her cellphone and took out a stack of talismans from under her pillow.

She spread them out like a folding fan and slowly waved it, looking at Maddie innocently.

She just knew that they would do something, which was why she had prepared everything before bedtime. The reason that she could not sleep was because she was excited to see how those paranormal beings would react once they saw her preparation.

"..."

Maddie felt like she was being challenged.

She was sure that if she went forward, she would be struck by lightning and maybe vanish into thin air.

So, she changed her target and suddenly lunged at Claire. Her movements were halted when she saw a whole line of animal plushies staring at her.

All of them had button eyes except for Bellina, but Maddie felt like they were looking at her like predators.

"I think these two are your colleagues maybe?" Corinne suddenly said and held up two dolls with horrified expressions.

Those two dolls were the ones that Claire turned into double dolls. One of them was the one who attacked Claire at the hallway and the other one was the one who tried to trick Corinne into giving her entry.

Maddie looked and her eyes widened, her whole body was trembling. She recognized those two dolls, she was wondering why they went missing.

She looked at Corinne, who was smiling brightly at her; except to her, Corinne looked like a she-devil who held her colleagues hostage.

The ghost dolls seemed to be looking at her, begging her to rescue them. But Maddie couldn't move from the spot that she was standing on.

"Oh, look. They look like they wanted you to join them. What do you say?" Corinne asked, smiling even wider.

In the end, Maddie hurried out the door with one thought screaming in her mind.

'They are such bullies!' Maddie thought as she stormed down the hallway.

Corinne merely looked at Maddie's direction and went back to scrolling on her phone.

CHAPTER 6

Maddie had never been treated this way before, she felt so embarrassed and mad at the same time that she needed to let this out, so she started to spam in the night round crew group chat.

Lola, who was also one of the train crew that made night rounds, saw what Maddie said. Both her and Maddie's role as night round crew was to make sure that all travellers were on schedule for bedtime.

She scoffed at what Maddie said and couldn't help herself from laughing at her co-worker, however, what she replied to Maddie was different from her mocking expression.

Aww. Maddie, I'm so sorry that you had to go through that. Hope you feel better.

Lola put her phone away before she ran late in making rounds.

Danny could hear the footsteps coming down the hallway.

He had always been a night owl, asking him to sleep at 9pm was impossible. He had been tossing and turning around ever since the lights went out.

When he heard the footsteps, his whole body froze, and he kept telling himself to sleep.

'You're asleep, you're asleep, you're asleep...' Danny mumbled in his head, eyes closed.

As he tried to force himself to sleep, he only felt himself getting more awake and the sound of the footsteps seemed to get louder.

That was when he remembered the coupon he got from the lucky draw wheel.

After Maddie left, Corinne felt like she should get to sleep... after she finished one more round of snake game.

Cutie Pie Princess has invited you to do a gift exchange.

When Corinne saw that notification pop up on her screen, she was stunned. Not because she got a gift exchange offer, she was stunned by the traveller's name.

She clicked accept and the person instantly spammed like ten messages right into her inbox.

Corinne scrolled down, skipping through all the 'Ahs', '!s', and GIFs.

Cutie Pie Princess: "Ahhhh!"

Cutie Pie Princess: "Thank you so much for accepting my gift exchange invitation!"

Cutie Pie Princess: "You're the only one who didn't reject me!"

Cutie Pie Princess: "And it was my last chance to send out an invitation! I only had three chances!"

Corinne rubbed her eyes, feeling slightly drowsy.

King of the World: "Do you need something in particular, Cutie Pie Princess?"

Cutie Pie Princess: "Yes, yes! Something to fend off the ghost!"

When Corinne saw what Cutie Pie Princess said, she thought that maybe Maddie or some other member of the train crew had made their rounds to her room. If that was the case, she knew exactly what Cutie Pie Princess needed.

Cutie Pie Princess: "But, I don't really have any items. The only thing I got from the Travel Agency is this gift exchange voucher."

Underneath that message was a picture with the things Cutie Pie Princess owned.

There was a PSP, some game cards, comics...

Behind all of those things was a wrapped burger that seemed to be untouched. When Corinne saw that burger, her stomach growled and she gulped.

King of the World: "I have something that will help you. I just want that burger. You haven't touched it right?"

Cutie Pie Princess: "..."

Cutie Pie Princess: "I mean, yeah!"

Once they reached an agreement, a screen appeared in front of Corinne. The title said 'Gift Exchange' and underneath the box letters were two boxes.

The box on the left had Corinne's traveller name beneath it and a 'Confirm' button.

The box on the right already had a wrapped burger in it and on top of the box it said 'Triple Cheese Chicken Burger.'

Corinne threw in some lightning tempest talismans and when the items were in the box, she tapped confirm.

After she did that, the items switched places and the screen vanished. The burger magically appeared out of thin air and dropped into Corinne's hand.

Cutie Pie Princess: "Thank you so much!"

King of the World: "No problem."

Corinne looked at the burger in her hand and started unwrapping it. When she heard Claire turning in her bed, she flinched. Claire always nagged her about how unhealthy it was to eat something late in the night.

She stole a glance at Claire and was relieved to see that she was still sound asleep despite everything that was going on.

While Corinne happily ate the burger, she could not help but think how nice Cutie Pie Princess was; she must be a cute and kind girl. She did hope that Cutie Pie Princess would do more gift exchanges with her, she would accept the request every time if she was offering more burgers.

Cock-a-doodle-do!

Corinne woke up to the piercing noise of the chicken clucking throughout their cabin.

Then, the curtains slid open on their own and the sharp morning rays slipped into their room, almost blinding Corinne.

"Gah!" Corinne sat up, throwing a fit on the bed, annoyed by the noise.

She glanced at the clock on the wall, it was 8am sharp. Claire was up as well. In contrast to Corinne, who was looking mad, she was in a daze. She rubbed her eyes and sniffed.

"Uh... why do I smell cheeseburger?" she asked.

Corinne's grumpiness from having her sleep interrupted was gone instantly, she was about to change the subject when the clucking of the chicken was finally replaced by a familiar 'bzzz' sound.

"Good morning, fellow travellers! This is the morning news by Hell Travel Agency. First of all, we would like to announce the opening of Hell Express Six! It is already up and running. Our travellers will be getting off at their first station today! Let's hope Express Six Travellers enjoy their trip and stay alive. Oops, I mean have a safe trip!"

Corinne rolled her eyes upon hearing what the news anchor said. Those sly bastards, they were always up to something no good.

"On to the next news.

Congratulations Express Five Traveller, Bestselling Fantasy Author, for making Top One on Hell Express Five Traveller's Ranking, and for earning the title 'Bear Child Disiplinarator'.

A round of applause please.

Congratulations Express Five Traveller, Bestselling Romance Author, for earning the titles 'Everyone's Oppa' and 'Bear Child Disciplinarator Assistant'.

Another round of applause please.

That will be it for today's morning news. Have a great day everyone."

From the morning news, Corinne caught a few key pieces of information.

First, apart from Hell Express Six, which was the train she was on, there were other trains.

Second, there was actually a traveller's ranking board.

Third, travellers could earn titles.

She still didn't know whether there would be any benefits from taking the top ranks or titles.

But...

"I can't believe traveller's names will appear in the announcements..." Corinne said to Claire with a serious expression.

Claire blinked, then she remembered Corinne named herself 'King of the World'.

Claire burst out laughing just imagining one day everyone would hear Corinne's traveller name in the announcement.

Knock
Knock
Knock
Knock

"Breakfast?" Someone called out by the door.

Corinne repeated her actions from yesterday, threatening to lightning strike before politely placing her order.

She pulled out her cellphone to pay with her e-wallet, but the staff outside said they don't accept that currency anymore.

"Why?" Corinne asked.

"You have officially registered as a traveller. We only take traveller points now."

Corinne tapped on the app, and after scanning the QR code, she stared at her phone in shock.

Checking the balance in her traveller wallet showed: -55 points

"..."

Corinne could not believe what she just saw, she hadn't even figured out how she could earn points and she was already in debt!

Seeing Corinne all mopey, Claire patted her on the head.

"Don't worry, I bet we'll get plenty of points when we finish our trip at the first station. The titles the other travellers earned probably gave them points as well," Claire said.

"You mean I can try to become 'Everyone's Oppa' too?" Corinne asked with a serious look.

"Uh..." Claire had no idea how to respond to that question.

"Hey, the waffles look so tasty."

"Oh, really? Wow, smells nice," Corinne instantly redirected her attention to the food.

'Works every time,' Claire thought.

"Don't think that I don't know you're changing the subject by talking about food," Corinne said, taking a bite of her own waffle.

CHAPTER 7

When the time hit 10AM, a screen appeared in front of Corinne.

Next Station: Cakeland Kingdom

A red button with block letters that said 'Start' was flashing on the screen.

Corinne and Claire exchanged a glance as they nodded. Both of them clicked on the button and Corinne saw that her passport flipped open, and the stamp that represented Cakeland Kingdom appeared on the page.

The stamp flashed a blinding white light, causing Corinne to pull down her rose-coloured sunshades from her hair and close her eyes at the same time.

When Corinne opened her eyes again, she found herself standing in the middle of a town square, surrounded by buildings that were made from various types of pastries and candies.

A few feet away from her was a chocolate fountain. A human statue holding a cake wand stood on top of the fountain and rainbow sprinkles rained down from the wand.

'Cakeland Kingdom...' this thought flashed in Corinne's mind.

There were several people standing in the town square as well. Some looked wary while glancing around, whereas others just looked scared.

Claire was standing right beside the fountain. Corinne was about to walk towards her when the ground shook.

'Earthquake?' she thought, just before a shadow loomed over her.

A red, scaly dragon just stomped on a house and swiped its tail at them.

"Dodge!" Corinne cried, and back flipped herself to the fountain, distancing herself from the dragon.

Claire did the same thing and now, both of them were standing on the fountain, holding onto the human statue to balance themselves.

With Claire by her side, Corinne knew she had her back, so she took the chance to quickly look around their surroundings, searching for an escape route and a place to hide.

When they arrived at Cakeland Kingdom, the sun was already going down. Besides the other people with them here in the town square, the entire place seemed desolate, as if they were the only ones here.

Darkness painted the sky until one of the buildings in the distance lit up. It stood out among all the other dessert buildings with its huge LED shop sign that said 'Cakeland Cafe'.

"Ah! Help!"

A person screamed, struggling to break free from the gripping tail of the dragon to no avail.

Before anyone could help that guy, the dragon tossed him up into the air and swallowed him.

Seeing that happen, everyone panicked and picked up their pace at running.

"Everyone! Run towards Cakeland Cafe!" Corinne cried.

She ran as fast as she could after screaming that to the other travellers, she didn't know whether they heard her or not, but with that building being the only one with lights on, it was a clear direction for them, an obvious landmark.

The dragon chased after them, crashing and knocking down the buildings that were in its way.

"Ah!"

Hearing a scream, Corinne instinctively looked behind her while she continued to run.

Two guys were behind her, a guy with paler skin, who looked like he might have tripped and fell on the ground while a second guy with tan skin was helping him up.

When pale skin guy got up, the tan guy was practically dragging him as he ran. Corinne glanced at the dragon and then at their speed, the dragon would catch up to them any second.

She bit her lower lip and paused for only a heartbeat before she started running toward the two of them.

"Corinne!" Claire cried.

"You go! I'm going to help them!" Corinne said, not slowing down at all.

Being Corinne's best friend, Claire knew that Corinne couldn't leave someone who needed help behind, and she wasn't going to leave her alone to face the monster. She turned around to chase after Corinne.

A guy in a blue shirt ran past them, storming towards the cafe. He was running speedily, but Claire still caught the flash of a wicked expression on his face. Claire narrowed her eyes as she looked over her shoulder, glaring at the guy's retreating figure.

Corinne caught up to the two guys. The pale guy was panting heavily, looking like he was about to pass out any second. The tan guy attempted to pick him up, but he didn't have enough strength.

Seeing that the dragon was closing in, Corinne dashed over, turning her back to the pale guy.

"Quick! Hop on!" she said.

The pale guy didn't even hesitate, he jumped onto Corinne's back and circled his arms around Corinne's shoulders.

Dumbfounded, the tan guy was about to gasp in surprise when he felt himself being picked up by Corinne like a puppy.

The dragon growled angrily seeing that Corinne stormed off at the speed of lightning even though she was carrying two guys that were taller than her.

It lunged at Corinne, the tan guy squeaked like a timid mouse and threw a talisman at the dragon.

When the talisman hit the monster, a lightning bolt struck down, but it did not cause any damage to the dragon at all.

Corinne raised a brow when she saw the talisman. It looked exactly the same as her lightning tempest talisman, she could sense her spiritual energy in it.

'Cutie Pie Princess?' she thought silently.

Claire summoned her needle and thread, directing them towards the dragon. The needle flew towards the dragon as silvery thread began to circle around it, trying to wrap the dragon in a cocoon.

The dragon ran through the threads as though they never existed. Seeing that her attack did not work, Claire instantly summoned her weapon back without a second thought.

Corinne and Claire exchanged a glance, shock flashed through their eyes. They had no idea why their attacks didn't work on the mighty beast.

Lightning tempest talisman might have been most effective on ghosts and spirits, but that didn't mean that it wouldn't work on monsters too, which was why Corinne was shocked to see that it didn't even cause a scratch on the dragon.

Pushing down the confusion, Corinne picked up her pace and ran at full speed.

When they stormed into the café, the other travellers were already in there. Some of them let out relieved sighs when they saw them, while others worriedly glanced out to see whether the dragon was there or not.

However, they were all dumbstruck by how easy it was for Corinne to carry two guys while fleeing from the dragon and doing so without breaking a sweat. Claire knew that Corinne had inhuman strength, so it was an easy task for her.

Claire snuck a glance at the guy in the blue shirt. He was taken aback when he saw them and there was panic in his eyes. This made Claire even more apprehensive; the blue shirt guy was acting very suspicious.

As soon as they were inside the cafe, the door slammed shut. The dragon that was charging towards them halted in place as soon as the door was closed.

Both of the guys she had been carrying thanked Corinne for her help just before all the travellers' attention were pulled to the screens that appeared in front of them.

Ding!

[Station: Cakeland Kingdom

Cakeland Kingdom had been producing many tasty treats for centuries until a dragon awakened in their land and started attacking the kingdom.

The Kingdom sent many brave warriors to slay the dragon to no avail, until a pâtissier came to the kingdom. Everyone was surprised that the kingdom was saved by a pâtissier that only know how to make tasty treats.

Being the hero of Cakeland Kingdom, he became the royal pâtissier in the castle. The dragon was not slain however. Instead, he was put into a deep slumber by the pâtissier using a pastry that he enchanted with a magical wand that had been passed down in his family for generations.

Every ten years, the pâtissier would make a tasty dessert and cast a spell on the treat before serving it to the dragon.

The dragon could not refuse a delicious treat made by the highly skilled pâtissier and would hibernate once again after it ate.

Things went smoothly until monsters around the kingdom started attacking small towns and villages at the outskirts of Cakeland Kingdom.

The King noticed treats made using the pâtissier's recipe could calm down the monsters and decrease their desire to kill. Hence, multiple Cakeland Cafes were built around the outskirts of Cakeland Kingdom.

That year, the dragon awakened from hibernation and the royal pâtissier was supposed to put the dragon back to sleep.

Unfortunately, the wand had been lost, and the treat served without the spells did not work. The royal pâtissier failed his mission and is now dead.

Now, the Kingdom's hope falls on the royal pâtissier's heir, his only daughter who is recuperating at the pâtissier's homeland.

Mission: Find the lost wand and put the dragon back to hibernation.

Identity: You are the staff of the Cakeland Cafe at the Kingdom's capital.]

When everyone finished taking in the information from the screen, their respective screens closed.

"I believe everyone has finished reading the information for this station. Why don't we start by introducing ourselves? I'm Ava and this is my sister, Mia."

Corinne looked over and saw that the speaker was a tall, beautiful woman with an hourglass body. She had short hair and a pair of fierce fox-like eyes that hid behind a pair of glasses. She held out her hand, pointing towards the woman standing next to her as she made the introduction.

"Hello, everyone," greeted the second woman, Ava's sister, Mia.

In contrast to Ava, who gave out a mature and intelligent vibe, Mia seemed cheerful, with high pigtails and a gleaming smile.

When it was the pale guy's turn to make his introduction, Corinne stood there, frozen like a statue, with her eyes widened in shock as the guy spoke.

His face turned beet red when he noticed everyone's eyes were on him, and he flashed a soft, timid smile.

"I'm Quinn."

Corinne's hand went over and pulled Claire's sleeve tightly.

Earlier, due to everything happening so fast, Corinne barely noticed the appearance of the guy and when they got to the cafe, her attention was grabbed by the introduction of their current station.

"Cl-Cl-Claire, am I dreaming? Why is Prince Florian standing right in front of me?" Corinne mumbled in a soft, stuttering voice that only Claire could hear.

Claire was as surprised as Corinne. This guy looked exactly like the visual novel character that Corinne was obsessed with.

Everyone's gazes had already moved on to the next person who was introducing himself, everyone except for Corinne that is.

When Quinn noticed Corinne staring at him, he shifted his eyes away with blushing cheeks, but recalling that she was the one who saved him earlier, he moved his eyes back and gave her a friendly smile.

Corinne sucked in a deep breath and felt like she was going to pass out from that shiny smile.

Claire squeezed Corinne's cheek, "Get it together!"

CHAPTER 8

When everyone finished making their introductions, Corinne got everyone's names from Claire. The tan guy was Danny and the guy in the blue shirt was Perry.

Growl!

A loud grumble shook the air as the earth beneath them shuddered as if struck by an earthquake.

Looking towards the window, Corinne flinched when she saw the red dragon's eyes staring at them through the glass.

"Guys, look!" Mia called out.

When they walked over, they saw eight rectangular tags on the table.

"Please select a name tag to confirm your role in the cafe," Ava read the paper in her hand aloud.

The dragon growled, trying to barge into the building, but the cafe stood strong. Corinne narrowed her eyes and then something clicked in her head.

"We should quickly choose a name tag," Corinne said and grabbed one.

Everyone followed suit and Perry clipped the name tag with the word 'chef' on his shirt.

As soon as he put on the name tag, his blue shirt and white washed jeans were replaced by a chef's uniform.

"What did you guys get?" Danny asked, "I got chef. What should I do? I don't know how to cook."

Danny looked down, before he got onto this haunted train, he had led a privileged, wealthy life. He had Michelin chef that cooked for him, maids and butlers who tended to his everyday needs. The only thing he knew how to cook was probably cup noodles, which didn't really require any cooking skills at all, just the ability to pour hot water into the cup.

"Don't worry, I'll help you," Perry said, "or you can be my assistant in the kitchen."

Danny gave him a wide, fake smile; he didn't really trust Perry. He might have thought that nobody realized what he did earlier, but Danny clearly saw him tripping Quinn, just so someone could slow the dragon down.

"I got server. Claire, what did you get?" Corinne asked and glanced at Claire's name tag.

"Same," Claire said with a smile.

"Mine is bartender," Ava said and clipped her name tag on.

Her clothing changed. Her knee-length skirt turned into black fitted pants, her heels changed into a pair of leather shoes, her top was replaced by a white, buttoned-up shirt with black vest, and a cute apron graced her hips and waist.

"What about you?" Ava asked Mia.

Mia turned her name tag for everyone to see. Her face turned as white as a ghost and her lips quivered.

[Security]

Stunned, everyone went quiet because they knew what being security meant.

The system said the existence of the cafe was to serve food to the monsters that attempted to infiltrate the kingdom.

If a chef needed to prepare food, a bartender made beverages, and server waited tables, what did that leave for security to do?

Obviously, it had something to do with the monsters. The position of a security guard must have been the most dangerous among all the positions.

Ava saw how pale Mia's face was and felt her heart tighten, Mia was her little sister. Even though neither of them were newbie travellers, she knew that Mia was not proficient in combat.

"Mia, let's exchange name tags," Ava said.

"Sis..." Mia said, her grip around the name tag tightened, but she shook her head.

How could she put her sister in danger? She was the one who got this name tag.

"There's one more on the table, why don't you take that?" Danny said and grabbed the one on the table.

When he turned the name tag around to see what it said, his mouth twitched.

[Security]

The hope that had risen in Mia's heart dropped back when she saw it.

"Take my name tag," Ava said, trying to take off her own name tag.

[Warning! Exchanging positions is forbidden.]

Everyone saw the warning screen that popped out above Ava's head.

"Once we put on the name tag, our position must have confirmed," Claire said.

"Sis, it's okay. We all picked our name tags randomly, I will try my best to do my role," Mia said, forcing a smile.

"Mia..." Ava looked at her younger sister, her eyes filled with concern.

Both of them were immersed in a pool of sorrow, when a hand appeared in front of them, a 'server' tag sitting on the palm of the small hand.

Glancing up, they saw Corinne flashing a bright smile.

Startled, they blinked. Corinne pushed the 'server' tag into Mia's arms and took the 'security' tag from the table, putting it on.

"Wait, you don't have to do th—" Mia tried to stop Corinne, but the brunette's outfit was already transformed.

The uniform fit Corinne as if it were tailored to her, the hem of the jacket coming to a perfect horizontal line at her waist, the shirt buttoned up the front, with a tiny collar and cuffs that looked like they were made out of a stiff leather. The pants were black and outlined with a thin strip of gold that snaked from hip to knee to ankle.

"I'm so sorry," Mia apologized.

Corinne looked at how guilty both Ava and Mia were and gave them a reassuring smile.

"You don't have to be sorry," she explained. "I think that each position is important in running Cakeland Cafe. And with the warning earlier stating that we cannot exchange positions, I can't imagine what would happen if a position became vacant."

"But..." Mia said.

Ava stopped Mia and shook her head. Nobody wanted to risk their own life, so if Corinne was volunteering as security, she must have some tricks up her sleeve.

"Mia is my sister and no matter what your purpose is, I still appreciate your action. I don't have much to offer, but here," Ava said.

Corinne looked at Ava and her genuine smile, then at the item that was given to her.

[Spicy Pepper Spray (made by Chef Gordon, distributed by Hell Travel Agency)

Pepper that is so spicy that it might cause blindness and there is a small probability of causing paralysis.

Spray count: 5]

The pepper spray looked like a plastic, see-thru mist bottle. It felt light and empty. If the system did not show the spray count, Corinne would have thought that it was an empty bottle.

Perry, who had been watching by the sidelines, secretly let out a sigh of relief. Being a chef was definitely better than security. Luckily, he already clipped the name tag. Seeing how excessively naive the brunette was he couldn't help but sneer.

He looked at Quinn, he had innocent and delicate features, with a pair of clear, shiny, almond shaped eyes. He might be a guy, but Perry was certain that his beauty exceeded everyone's in this room.

Quinn was merely wearing a plain white t-shirt with a brown cardigan over it and a pair of dark blue jeans, a casual outfit, but he looked like an aristocrat.

His eyes went from Quinn to Corinne. A naive girl with an overflowing sense of justice and a feeble pretty boy, he already assumed that they might be the first to die.

He turned back to Quinn, mockingly gazed at him up and down, not even bothering to hide how he felt.

"What about you? What did your tag say?" Perry asked and pulled at the name tag in Quinn's hand.

Quinn, not expecting Perry's sudden movement, lost his footing. He let out a 'yelp' and his hands were waving around trying to grab something to balance himself.

When Quinn thought that he would fall, he shut his eyes waiting for the pain that was to come. Then, he felt a pair of small hands on his arms. He opened his eyes and a pair of clear, gleaming eyes locked with his gaze.

"Careful," Corinne said.

Under Corinne's strong grip, Quinn balanced himself.

A faint blush painted his cheeks as he muttered, "Thank you."

"Hey! I saw what you did, don't you think you should apologize?" Danny said, "Earlier, you made Quinn fall to slow down the dragon so you could escape and now you tried to make him trip again?"

"I don't know what you're talking about, do you have any proof?" Perry shrugged.

"Quinn, is that true?" Corinne asked.

Quinn bit his lower lip, glancing at Perry briefly. When Perry glared at him, he flinched, and his grip tightened on Corinne's sleeve.

"Don't glare at Quinn!" Danny cried.

"Are you threatening Quinn?" Mia puffed up her cheeks.

Looking at Quinn's glassy eyes and quivering lips, Corinne couldn't help but pat Quinn on his hand, giving him an encouraging gaze.

"Don't be scared," Corinne said.

Danny and Mia also came up to Quinn and comforted him.

Quinn looked at them, touched.

"Thank you, guys. I'm not looking for anyone to blame and it is certainly not Perry's fault, my health has always been poor, and I have a frail body that causes me to lose my balance and trip... I'm such a weakling," Quinn's words ended with yet another sob.

Seeing the tears that were about to flow down Quinn's cheek and how pale his face was, Corinne, Danny, and Mia instantly felt a mild heart ache. They glared at Perry and then went back to comfort Quinn.

"..."

Claire and Ava exchanged a glance. They could see the disbelief in each other's eyes.

Hmmm...

How should they put it? Quinn wasn't being rude or anything.

But the way he said it...

Looking at Quinn's every act and move, how he could muster up the tears in his eyes within seconds and make it look like they were about to flow down, the way he angled his face, and how he made himself look innocent and weak. None of it seemed sincere.

Perry's jaw dropped when he saw how Quinn was acting.

In the end, after everyone put on their name tags, the dragon left, and someone suddenly stepped forward.

"Dinner is ready."

Chapter 9

"Please step over to the dining area."

Everyone stared, shocked, at the man that appeared out of nowhere and was now standing in front of them.

The man wore an expensive looking suit, his hair was pulled back into a slick, neat cut, his face had little to no expression, and a tiny pair of spectacles sat on the bridge of his nose.

Corinne and the others exchanged glances before they trailed behind the man that looked like a butler.

The butler led them to the dining area and Corinne could smell the tasty aroma of well-prepared food as soon as she stepped into the room.

The long wooden table with checkered tablecloth was set with the most delicious-looking food. Corinne's eyes lit up, she was hungry, and her stomach rumbled.

"Is it raining? I think I heard thunder," Danny asked.

"..."

Flustered, Corinne was about to retort when she saw how genuine Danny's expression looked.

"I thought that was the sound of the dragon coming back," Mia said, looking as sincere as Danny.

"..."

Claire looked at Corinne, who stood beside her, looking all flushed, and laughed.

"That is just Corinne's stomach," Claire said.

Corinne puffed up her cheeks, her whole face exploded in red. "Yup... it's my stomach."

The others tried to hold back their laughter so much that their faces were as red as tomatoes.

Corinne gave them a glare before she pulled up a chair and got herself seated.

The man in the butler suit coughed, grabbing their attention.

"I'm Lady Eloise's butler, Owen." The butler introduced himself after everyone was seated.

"I am here on behalf of Lady Eloise, as she is busy preparing the slumber magic dessert to express our gratitude for you all volunteering in the search for the lost wand. Please enjoy the dinner and rest for the night." Owen gestured to the dinner on the dining table.

He proceeded to set down the room keys as he spoke, "Tomorrow, we will need to enter the palace to meet with the prince before the cafe opens. The rooms are on the second floor of this building."

"Before I leave, there is one thing I wanted to let you all know. Even if you have a valid identity in the Kingdom as cafe staff, it is still dangerous out there. Now, please excuse me." With that being said, Owen left the room.

Corinne hadn't taken her eyes off the food since she sat down, and now she gulped. As soon as Owen was out of sight, her hands flew across the table to fill up her plate.

"Is the food safe to eat?" Mia muttered to her sister.

Her voice was low, almost like a whisper, but for those who were cautiously staring at the food in front of them, they all heard what she said.

"Well…" Ava said.

Her eyes went over to Corinne and Danny.

When Corinne's cheeks puffed up just like a squirrel because of all the food she stuffed in her mouth, she realized that all eyes were on her.

Danny was sitting beside her; he had the same bulged up cheeks and identical mountain-sized stack of food on his plate as

Corinne. Both of their gazes met, and Danny swallowed and flashed a wide grin.

Corinne did the same before she started to speak, "When we were running away from the dragon, the streets were empty, and all the houses looked vacant. It is not fully dark yet, but none of the lights are on anywhere else, only at this cafe.

"Our mission goal is to find the lost wand and also to put the dragon back to sleep. Unless this is some sort of survival stage, I think the food should be safe to consume.

"If not, before we find the wand, we could starve to death."

Corinne curled the spaghetti using the fork in her hand as she glanced up, "Plus, Danny and I are fine, aren't we?"

Claire was the first to react, she grabbed a sandwich in front of her. She was just as hungry as Corinne, but she was cautious. The minute she did not pay attention to Corinne, her bestie was gobbling down the food.

She didn't manage to stop Corinne, and luckily, she was fine. Knowing Corinne for so long, Claire knew that the girl might have looked like she did not have a care in the world, but in reality, she was sensitive and observant.

When everyone finished their meal, each of them picked a key and went to the second floor.

The rooms were small, with a simple bed, an attached bathroom, a bedside table, and a large window.

Corinne noticed that everything inside the room was made of pastries, just like the building itself.

She went closer to the bed; the bed was made from soft cake and the lamp was made from glass candy. Moving to the window, she saw the sun set right before her eyes and darkness quickly painted the entire place.

A dim light lit up the room, then the sound of growling and stomping filled the streets.

The empty streets were suddenly filled with monsters. They swarmed the streets, some were small and unknown, while others were huge and terrifying. They came from every direction, their eyes glowing red in the darkness. All the monsters were just mindlessly roaming the streets.

Corinne remembered what Owen said earlier and also how the dragon that was chasing after them left when they all put on the name tags.

That was it.

Identity.

When they arrived at the kingdom, they didn't have any identities until they put on the name tags. The dragon left when they became employees at the cafe.

The kingdom's cafe staff provided food for the monsters during business hours and the monsters stopped attacking the kingdom.

It was like the kingdom and the monsters reached some sort of silent agreement.

With Owen's warnings about the risks of wandering out at night, Corinne wondered what those risks would be. Seeing the beasts that wandered about at night, Corinne confirmed that even with their cafe staff identity, if the beasts caught them at night, it would be extremely dangerous.

Thinking about the day's events, Corinne began to stick her talismans all over the room before going to bed. She thought she would have a hard time falling asleep because of the running thoughts in her mind, but surprisingly, she fell into a deep slumber almost immediately.

Ring

Ring

Ring

Under the sound of the ringing bells, Corinne woke up. She looked at the door and window to check whether any talismans had been disturbed. Once she saw that all of them were still in place, she took a deep breath and relaxed.

She quickly surveyed the room, and only when she was certain that all the talismans weren't used did she start moving again. When those talismans were placed, she cast an incantation, the talismans would have been activated if they detected danger. Once the talismans were used, the spiritual energy that was infused in them would diminish.

Corinne moved towards the window and looked outside; she did not see a single monster. The streets remained empty, though. It was as if the town was abandoned, and they were the only ones here.

She waved her hand, and all the talismans glowed a soft gold as they flew into her hands. After putting away each talisman, she prepared herself to go downstairs.

She opened the door and her eyes lit up when she saw Claire, both of them exchanged a glance and moved closer to each other.

"None of my talismans were activated last night," Corinne stated.

"Same here, and Bellina did not see anything," Claire mentioned.

Bellina didn't need to sleep at all, so she was perfect to be on guard duty at night. After listening to Claire's words, Corinne was certain that they should be safe as long as they stayed in their room.

When Corinne saw the other travellers at the dining table, she was reassured that nothing had happened the night before because everyone seemed perfectly fine. Claire sauntered in last, and Corinne looked at the butler from last night standing in the corner with a bell made from glass. When she looked closer, she noticed that the bell was actually made from sugar glass.

The ringing sound she heard earlier must have been from Owen's bell. When Corinne sat down next to a few other travellers after taking in the scene, she noticed that none of them looked anxious. Instead, all of them were relaxed and unconcerned; it was as if they had all gotten a full night's rest.

It was either like what Corinne thought, nobody tried to break in last night, or they all masked their expressions. Corinne couldn't think of anything beneficial that could come from doing that though. With the name tags that decided their respective roles and also their shared goals, they should have been working together.

It was only the first day, she didn't even see the *important NPCs* yet. Corinne calmed her racing mind and directed her attention to the food in front of her.

At the same time, when Owen saw that everyone was at the table, he rang the small, sugar glass bell in his hand again to gain everyone's attention.

"Breakfast will be at the same time every day," he said. "In addition, as I need to be by Lady Eloise's side and my work here is done, I have arranged for a carriage to take us to our meeting. Please finish your breakfast. We do not want to be late for the meeting with the prince."

Owen bowed his head, then stood by the door like a doorman while the travellers finished eating.

Chapter 10

"You guys must be the cafe staff that volunteered to search for the wand."

Corinne stared at the sight in front of her, her mouth hung open in shock. After they finished breakfast, they had been sent to the castle in a carriage.

The palace, like all buildings in Cakeland Kingdom, was made out of desserts. It looked like a giant dream of a gingerbread house that was made of a thousand differently coloured tiles, the palace was gorgeous and magnificent. The palace guards, who were all gingerbread men, wielded candy canes and patrolled the walls day and night.

"A pleasure to finally meet you, I am Lady Eloise."

Two stunningly beautiful women with dazzling eyes and flawless skin smiled at them. They were wrapped in luxurious gowns that trailed behind their heels when they walked.

What stunned Corinne was not how strikingly attractive the two young women were, but they looked exactly alike, like twins. The only difference was the colour of their clothing and accessories. One was completely dressed in black, the other all in white. Then she noticed there were also two versions of Owen, similarly dressed in black and white.

Owen in the black suit, who had ushered them into the palace, went over to black-dressed Eloise, who sat in her seat, holding a cup of steaming hot tea. Black Eloise smiled at them as a greeting, but did not get up from her seat, choosing instead to continue sipping her tea.

Her gown was a shimmering black silk, tight and form fitting with no adornment other than a black velvet ribbon tied into a bow gracing her waist.

The Lady Eloise dressed in white had been the one to introduce herself, smiling warmly. Her gown, also of the finest silk, was draped and cut to accentuate her every curve, gleaming in the purest white.

Corinne looked at the butler that was by White Eloise's side. He had the same appearance as the Owen that was with them, but this man wore a white suit, an exact colour match with White Eloise.

Under the sound of a blowing horn and rainbow sprinkles raining down from the sky, a heavy door swung open to reveal a teenage boy who entered the room with his own background music playing.

He was robed in a brilliant, twisting cloak of purple fabric, lined with sapphire and amethyst. Gold-plated buckles held his cloak together, and a thick belt of gold and silver circled his waist. Even though he was adorned by valuable gemstones, nothing could outshine his crown, a golden band set with a glittering ruby in the center.

Corinne pulled down her rose-colored sunshades because she thought a walking treasure chest just walked into the room.

"Wow, way to make an entrance," Danny muttered.

His voice was barely a whisper, but when the prince walked by, he delivered a cold stare that caused Danny to flinch, and his hands flew up to cover his mouth.

"The passing of the royal pâtissier was very unfortunate," the prince said, taking a sip of hot cocoa. "Since then, the dragon has endangered the people in our kingdom. Cakeland Kingdom is blessed that so many of you are willing to search for the wand left by the pâtissier. Please continue to manage the cafe while participating in this search."

Before anyone could speak, White Eloise went to the front of the room and curtsied before she spoke. "Your majesty," she said, respectfully.

"When the wand is retrieved, I will certainly follow in my father's footsteps to protect the kingdom." White Eloise smiled at the prince as her cheeks turned red; she stole a glance at him from the corner of her eye.

"It is my duty as the daughter of the royal pâtissier, therefore I will fulfill my part in putting the dragon back into deep slumber and restore the peace of Cakeland Kingdom," Black Eloise said.

She did not steal glances at the prince like White Eloise; instead, she stood with her back ramrod-straight, both her hands were placed on her abdomen, and her gaze was lowered slightly without meeting the prince's eyes.

After hearing what the two Eloises said, the prince finally let a smile show on his face. His eyes got warm, softened, and he looked at them in a new way. "It's a pleasure to have you with us," he told the two Eloises.

Feeling the prince's gaze on them, White Eloise blushed while Black Eloise remained calm.

"Now, all we need to do is get the wand and we can bring back the peaceful kingdom for our people," he said.

The prince set down his cup and turned to the travellers. Following his gaze, the rest of the people in the room turned to look at them as well. Corinne flinched and instinctively took a step forward, wanting to mimic the Eloises and curtsy, but when she remembered she was in a security uniform, she recalled how the butler had bowed and did that in front of the prince instead.

"Oh! Great Prince of the Cakeland Kingdom!"

As soon as Corinne opened her mouth, Claire's eyes twitched, and the others' jaws dropped watching Corinne's theatrical performance.

The prince coughed and delicately brought his cup back to his twitching lips. He took a small sip, then set it down.

"We, who are loyal to the Cakeland Kingdom, will do everything we can to fulfill our duties and protect the Kingdom from the evil clutches of the dragon and recover the royal pâtissier's wand to bring back the peace and harmony of the kingdom. So that, the residents..." Corinne continued her performance.

When Corinne finished her five-thousand-word long speech, White Eloise had already dozed off, Black Eloise was still trying her best to maintain her lady-like posture, and the prince's smile had become strained.

"Very well, I will leave you to it then, wouldn't want to take up much of your time as you still need to tend the café." The prince stood up and walked towards the door.

Claire noticed that, although the prince maintained his graceful posture, his quick pace and retreating figure indicated that he couldn't stand to stay here any longer and was escaping from Corinne.

"Oh, Great Prince of Cakeland Kingdom, may I have another word please?"

The prince halted, he almost slipped from hearing Corinne's dramatic and loud voice, luckily, he managed to balance himself in time and saved himself from embarrassment.

"Of course," the prince responded through practically gritted teeth.

When Corinne saw that the prince turn back to face her, she gave him a beaming smile.

"The search for the royal pâtissier's wand is a task, an adventure, a journey that will bring risks and dangers upon our lives. However, as loyal members and residents of Cakeland Kingdom. We will definitely do everything we can, in order to…"

Hearing how Corinne was again starting her little dramatic performance, the prince sighed internally and rubbed the bridge of his nose, putting up a hand to stop the girl from giving another five-thousand-word speech.

"What do you want?"

Corinne blinked, "Some authority to freely enter places, investigate, and ask questions to gather information in relation to the royal pâtissier and the wand."

The prince peered his eyes at the girl, who gave him a harmless smile as though she was an obedient student. Feeling his gaze upon her, the girl returned it with her own bright eyes and even flashed her pearly whites.

When the others heard Corinne's request, all of them held their breath, except for Quinn. Quinn stood behind Danny and watched everything by the sidelines, silently.

His lips curled up, his eyes sharp and cold, the innocence from before was gone and replaced by a merciless glint.

'Interesting...' Quinn thought as he continued to observe Corinne.

When Corinne ran towards them with a round chocolate medal in her hand, Quinn lowered his gaze, his long lashes shadowed his eyes, and when he looked up, his eyes were once again clear and innocent.

Corinne looked at the round, chocolate medal that was handed to her by the prince's man.

Her heart was pounding, she had been so nervous when she spoke up to the prince.

They really had zero clues and no information about the wand except for the fact that the wand was something that was passed down for generations in the royal pâtissier's family and it went missing when the royal pâtissier died.

Things got even more confusing with two Eloises showing up and also, if they found the wand who should they give the wand to? Which Lady Eloise is the real one? Which of them is the real daughter?

The prince had reacted normally in front of the Eloises. Having no clues about the whereabouts of the wand or why there were two Eloises, Corinne was going to get a major headache because of this mess.

But first things first, searching for the wand would be top priority. Black Eloise and White Eloise seemed to be living in the palace. Since they were doing this for Cakeland Kingdom, it would be natural for them to gain some assistance from the prince right?

It didn't take long for Corinne to decide and risk it by asking the prince. Luckily, the situation ended up on a positive note.

When Corinne joined the rest of the group, the others gave her a thumbs up, except for Perry, who looked at the medal greedily with a frown.

The others were just happy that Corinne got that because it would definitely be helpful for their quest.

Without wasting anymore time, they hurried back to the cafe for the opening.

Ding Ling Ling

The sound of the ringing bells signaled that the cafe was open for business. Corinne stared as the sign on the glass door turned to open.

[Please be at your own respective station and start your work.]

When the instruction popped out, Corinne saw a large red arrow pointing at the door. She walked over to the spot and stood by the door as monsters started to enter the cafe.

Danny and Perry were the chefs, both of them had already went into the kitchen. Ava was the bartender, in charge of making beverages. Quinn was the manager, and his position was at the cash register.

Claire and Mia needed to face the monsters directly because they needed to wait the tables. Claire was still okay, but Mia turned as pale as a ghost. Corinne could see that she was trembling as though she was in the north pole.

When the monsters sat down, Corinne could see a timer appear on top of their head as the monsters looked through the menu. The timer became a bell once they decided on what they wanted to order.

Claire proceeded to take their orders and the bell became a timer again until they got their orders.

Corinne looked at the others who were busy with their own tasks and felt confused. Was she just a doorman?

Seeing all the tables were full, Corinne had nothing to do at the moment and wanted to help out the others. But, when she moved to grab a tray, a huge exclamation mark appeared, halting her from her movement.

[Please remain at your position and strictly perform only your own tasks.]

'Does that mean if I'm security, I can only do tasks related to a security guard?' Corinne thought.

Brows raised, Corinne went back to her own spot.

Corinne just stood there until closing time, even Quinn worked more than her. Whenever a table finished, they would put their payments on the table and Quinn would collect them before heading back to the cash register.

Danny mentioned he didn't know how to cook, but the food that was served to the monsters seemed so delicious; maybe he was only helping Perry out while Perry was in charge in making all the dishes.

It was a torture for Corinne to just stand there with the tasty aroma of the food, knowing she could only see and was not able to eat.

Corinne stood there for hours with her stomach grumbling until the sound of the bell rang once again.

Ding Ling Ling

"Finally! I am starving!" Corinne exclaimed.

Claire and Mia, who had been walking around waiting tables and serving orders, heaved out sighs of exhaustion.

The kitchen crew—Danny and Perry—also came out from the kitchen to join the others, resting by the wood dining table.

"I can't wait for din-"

Corinne's words were cut off when an announcement popped out.

[Cakeland Cafe is closed for the day, but the monsters who had been waiting outside are not happy with the closing. Security needs to maintain the order of the crowd.]

Hearing that, everyone instantly turned towards Corinne.

Corinne peered out the window and sucked in a deep breath after she saw how many monsters were out there. The monsters were like sardines in a tin can. The bright light coming from the cafe caught the edges of the monsters' teeth, claws, and scaly hides, making a long black shadow stretch behind each beast.

Her skin tingled as if all of her nerves came to life, her stomach tightened, and her cheeks flushed, not from fear but excitement.

Okay, so her tasks literally start after the cafe is closed.

"Oh my god…" Mia gasped, as her lips quivered.

Everyone looked worried, even Perry.

[Security, please step out of the cafe to ease the tension of the crowd.]

The system was rushing Corinne at this point.

"Corinne, maybe you should take Bellina with you," Claire said.

Danny pulled out a couple of talismans and handed them over to Corinne.

Corinne shook her head, "Don't worry, I can still handle this."

Claire glanced out the window then back at Corinne, "Wait! On second thought, let me go with you."

"Me too," Ava said.

They tried to follow Corinne out the door, but as Corinne exited the cafe just fine, both of them seemed to hit an invisible wall.

"What's going on?" Claire asked, her hands touching some sort of force-field that prevented her from exiting.

"I guess only the security can go out because it is their task, just like how I cannot help you guys to wait tables because I'm not a server," Ava said.

Everyone filled up the space by the window and gazed out to watch from inside the cafe.

As soon as Corinne stepped out from the cafe, she reached for the golden chain around her neck. A pendant that looked like a sword was hanging on the chain. The sword pendant detached from the chain and became large.

The sword had been made from five emperor bronze coins, and when Corinne grabbed the hilt of the sword, it glowed with a soft golden energy.

Corinne took one step forward and all the monsters growled, dashing towards her.

"Bring it on!"

CHAPTER 11

"Lightning tempest!"

The talismans Corinne threw out formed a half circle in front of her and with a flick of her wrist, the talismans shot out, sticking on the monsters.

Then, lightning struck down and cleared out the monsters, forming an empty space in front of Corinne.

Corinne stormed forward with her sword; with all the monsters packed like a can of tuna, it was actually easier for Corinne to attack.

With a swing of her sword, Corinne sent out an energy wave, slashing the monsters in sight. Corinne had her talismans circle around her, forming a protective barrier.

No monsters could get near her, and whenever the monsters tried to sneak attack her, a talisman would automatically fly out and strike them with lightning.

When Corinne finished wiping out all the monsters that were causing a ruckus, she was drenched in blood—blood that was not her own, but the monster's.

"Has Corinne always been that strong?" Mia gasped, looking at Claire.

Claire did not say anything, and only responded with a smile.

Danny's eyes went wide, the talismans that Corinne used, they were the same as the ones he got from using the item exchange voucher.

Does that mean that Corinne was King of the World?

Wait... when he tried to give her the talisman... she recognized it, so did she know that he was Cutie Pie Princess?

She knew his embarrassing traveller's name!

At this moment, Danny just wanted to dig a hole and bury himself in it.

Danny averted his eyes when Corinne came in through the door, her sword turned back into a pendant and reattached on the gold chain.

"Corinne!" Claire rushed over. "Are you okay? Are you hurt anywhere?"

"Aside from being covered in blood and dirt, I'm fine," Corinne said with a wide grin.

[Cakeland Cafe

Status: Closed

Daily Quota: Good job at meeting the quota, keep it up!]

Not only Corinne was surprised by the screen that popped out, but the others were startled by the content as well.

Quota?

Did quota mean how many orders they made daily?

"Guys," Quinn called out.

Quinn was at the cash register, and he signaled for everyone to come over.

When everyone surrounded him, his face turned red as he tapped on the screen of the machine.

The screen showed the number of orders they made and also the total profit. Basically, a daily summary of the day of business.

Quinn proceeded to swipe up, bringing up the next screen.

"These popped up when the cafe closed for the day," Quinn said.

Corinne looked at the screen, it was options for them to upgrade or renovate the cafe.

They could select which appliances they wanted to upgrade; all the prices were listed below the selections.

"If we can level up the cafe, does that means the monsters will level up too?" Claire asked.

"No doubt about that," Ava said with her arms crossed. "The stations were always cunning; they would never let us complete our missions easily."

Perry squeezed himself between Corinne and Claire, pushing through them and heading straight for the screen, "Anyway…"

"We should really pick something to upgrade first, let's see…" Perry tried to swipe through the options, but a huge error popped up when his fingers made contact with the screen.

Perry cursed under his breath, and frowned at Quinn, "Tsk! I guess only the manager can work the cash register."

Corinne openly rolled her eyes at Perry and pushed him away to make space for herself and Claire.

"From the looks of it, we seem to have enough funds to choose two," Claire stated, after taking a look at the screen.

"I think it will be better for us to upgrade the kitchen and also the tables," Claire looked up, and asked to see what the others thought.

Ava nodded, "Yes, upgrading the kitchen can speed up the production of the food and the tables can increase customers' patience."

Seeing that everyone agreed on what to upgrade, Quinn proceeded to confirm the selections on screen.

A ring of light shot out from the screen, enveloping both the kitchen and the tables and chairs in the cafe. The sight of the glowing, ring-shaped light that surrounded the cafe furniture made everyone feel warm and fuzzy.

The tables and chairs that creaked and smelled of old dust had been replaced with new ones. The furniture in the cafe was made of pastries, and Corinne had no idea what pastries the tables became but the surface was polished and glaring under the light.

In the kitchen, the old equipment had been exchanged for new ones as well. All of them ruddy with newness. Everyone was in awe of the all-new appliances and furniture when Corinne's gasp caught their attention.

"Guys! We have a huge crisis!" Corinne cried.

"What?"

"What's wrong?"

Corinne pointed to the screen, everyone peered at what she tried to show them and was instantly at a loss of words.

The screen was showing the meal options and the prices for the food. Before this, Butler Owen was the one who offered them meals, but now they needed to pay for their meals using the funds they got from operating the cafe.

All of them briefly glanced at Corinne before they respectively went upstairs to their own rooms.

Claire was going to pat Corinne on the shoulder, but then her best friend was drenched in the blood of the monsters, so she patted Corinne on the head instead.

"Quickly go and wash up. After we eat, we still need to go out," Claire said before she went upstairs.

Dumbfounded, Corinne stood there as Claire and the others went upstairs to wash up after a day of hard work.

Head tilted a little to the side, Corinne was confused because she did not understand why everyone did not feel like this was a serious matter.

Corinne was definitely wrong about the others. Unlike her, some of them were not newbie travellers. They had spare food which they bought from the system shop and kept with them.

Even if they encountered a situation like insufficient funds to purchase food, they had others way to obtain it. The most important thing for them was to clear the station as soon as possible, so that they could leave this place and get back to the train.

Therefore, unlike the major foodie, Corinne, who worried that there was actually a possibility of not being able to get food, this really wasn't a huge thing for them at all.

"Don't worry, the food doesn't cost a lot, so I'm sure we would always have enough funds to enjoy a nice meal," Quinn said, his lips curled up into a warm smile.

Corinne felt so touched hearing his words.

"Let's work hard together!" Quinn said as his smile grew wider, putting his hands up in a 'we can do this' gesture.

"Yeah!" Corinne swooped in, grabbing Quinn's hands with fire in her eyes. "Let's do this!"

Quinn blinked as he watched Corinne dash away, fully motivated.

A string of low chuckles escaped his lips after brief seconds, shadows from his long lashes hiding the mischievous glints in his eyes.

CHAPTER 12

It was evening when Corinne headed straight for the palace. When they came this morning, Corinne did not take a close look at the exterior of the palace at all because they were in a hurry to prevent them from being late in meeting with the prince.

Seeing Cakeland Kingdom's castle right before her eyes, Corinne couldn't help but gape.

The castle looked like someone took a wedding cake and anchored it into the ground. The walls were made of fondant, champagne coloured with decorations and swirls that went around the castle. The towers looked like cupcakes with icing and sprinkles.

The entire palace was frilly and delicate and too sweet to be real, too pristine. Each tower was a different shape, but each was cut to precision. Each turret was a different color, but each a unique shade of pink or yellow.

The sweet smell of icing, butter, sugar, and a tad of frosting powder filled the air. Corinne's mouth watered as she stared at the castle, she could almost taste it.

Corinne walked towards the gate, she couldn't take her eyes off the towering castle that was made of refined sugar and sweets.

The gingerbread man guard that was by the gate stopped Corinne in her tracks, forcing her to briefly remove her eyes from the wall that looked a lot like strawberry cake and pull out the medal she got from the prince.

When the gingerbread man looked up from the medal and met Corinne's eyes, he instantly took a couple of steps back, putting his candy cane in front of his chest defensively.

The girl in front of him had a hungry glint in her eyes, making him feel like he was being served on a plate and brought to her.

When Corinne licked her lips, holding back the drool that desperately tried to escape her mouth, the guard instantly jumped away, sticking his back to the wall while holding up the candy cane.

Corinne was so confused as to why the guard was trembling like he would break into pieces. She was hungry, so she wanted to quickly get this over with and head back to the cafe.

Shrugging, Corinne stuffed the medal back into her pocket and picked up her pace. She needed to get back to the cafe before nightfall.

Corinne had a clear thought in her mind, she wanted to search the royal pâtissier's room and look through his belongings.

When Corinne was walking along the hallway trying to find someone that could point her to where she wanted to go, she heard chattering coming from a corner. She discreetly tiptoed towards the direction the sound came from.

Corinne hid herself behind a large vase of lollipop flowers and peered at the source of the chattering. It was two maids, one wearing a white maid outfit and the other one was in black.

Seeing the color of their dresses immediately reminded Corinne of Black Eloise and White Eloise.

"Poor Lady Eloise... not only did the royal pâtissier pass away, but she had to go through that tragic thunderstorm. Thankfully, even though the ship sunk, Lady Eloise survived..."

"I am worried about the wellness of Lady Eloise...I heard that she had been ill ever since she was a child, and the royal pâtissier's hometown was suitable for her recuperation, which was the reason why she had been staying there for so many years..."

"I see, if it weren't for the passing of the royal pâtissier, Lady Eloise would not have been summoned back to put the Dragon to sleep. I do hope Lady Eloise did not push herself too much, after all Lady Eloise's health is poor."

Lady Eloise was sick?

Corinne couldn't put the two Eloises she saw earlier in the day with the bedridden Eloise the maids' mentioned together.

Apart from the exceptional beauty that almost blinded Corinne, she really could not see a trace of being weak or ill from them.

Maybe they had recovered since then?

"I do hope the search party cafe staff are able to retrieve the lost wand, so Lady Eloise can bring back peace to the kingdom just like the royal pâtissier."

"Well, *my* Lady Eloise will definitely be able to complete her task. I don't know about *your* Lady Eloise though."

Hearing the mocking voice, Corinne was wide eyed over the maid in black suddenly being offensive.

"What do you mean? Anyone could see that *my* Lady Eloise is the real one," white maid crossed her arms, not backing down.

"Pffft, if they are blind that is. I will not discuss with you any further, I have finished sweeping the royal pâtissier's room and I'll be off to dust the study chamber now."

Corinne had watched the whole thing, the black maid and white maid were gossiping and seemed to be getting along, then things went downhill in such an unexpected turn.

But, thanks to them, Corinne knew where the royal pâtissier's chamber was, and their gossip actually gave out a lot of information.

When the two maids left, Corinne crept out from her hiding spot and headed straight for the dark chocolate door.

"Please be unlocked, please be unlocked..." Corinne muttered under her breath and turned the doorknob.

Click

Click

Click

Corinne's heart literally dropped when she heard the sound of clicking high heels coming from the other end of the corridor.

Thankfully, the door was unlocked, so Corinne speedily slipped into the room.

Her back was sticking to the door, and she was about to let out a sigh of relief when it got caught in her throat because...

The sound of the high heels just stopped, and it stopped right in front of the chamber door.

Corinne's eyes scanned through the entire chamber and then lit up when she spotted the perfect hiding place.

A shadow seeped in from underneath the door, Corinne gulped, praying that she wouldn't get caught.

Corinne stared at the shadow until it slowly went away. She listened to the sound of the clicking high heels go far off, until she couldn't hear it anymore.

Loosening up, she was about to jump down when the door to the chamber suddenly swung open. Corinne held her breath and paused all of her movement.

Corinne watched from her hiding spot as a tall woman in a maid's dress stepped in. Unlike the maids she saw earlier, this maid was in a black and white uniform.

The quality and design of the tall woman's uniform clearly showed that she had a higher rank than the normal maids.

She walked in, her hands were properly placed in front of her abdomen, and her every movement was like it was programmed. The distance between each of her steps was exactly the same.

The tall maid walked into the room without creating any sound. That was when Corinne realized that the clicking sound she heard earlier was made on purpose; the tall maid tried to deceive her.

Corinne watched silently as the tall maid suddenly opened the wardrobe, then knelt down to see underneath the bed and went over every single spot that could hide someone.

When she couldn't find anything, the tall maid began to exit the room, stopped briefly by the door, looking over her shoulder one last time before she stepped out from the room.

This time, Corinne waited a moment longer before she floated down from the ceiling. She was carried down by her paper figurines. Earlier, she whipped out a couple of them and had them carry her to the ceiling.

Corinne practically glued herself to a corner of the ceiling and stayed there the entire time the tall maid was roaming in the chamber.

Thankfully, the royal pâtissier's chamber had a high ceiling.

Corinne's eyes briefly swept over to the door before she started to search the former royal pâtissier's room.

Even though the royal pâtissier had passed away, the maids still cleaned his chamber, so everything in the chamber was still pretty neat and tidy except for the desk.

The desk stood out the chamber; it was hard for Corinne to not notice it with papers and books scattered on the table.

But what caught Corinne's attention the most was the framed photo sitting on the desk.

It was a family photo with only two people though, Corinne assumed that the guy in the picture is the royal pâtissier.

What surprised Corinne was the look of the girl in the picture. She was much younger than the two Elouises she met, must be a picture from earlier years.

The girl definitely had the exact same look as Black and White Eloise. But the impression of her was a lot different. She did not look like someone that was ill and was bedridden at all.

She was flashing a wide grin, and her eyes was as clear as the sky. Her skin was as pale as a snowflake, and her hair was gold and orange, like fire or the sun.

She looked cheerful and vibrant; her whole vibe was totally different from the two Elouises Corinne met earlier in the day.

Black Eloise looked proper, graceful, and reserved, whereas White Eloise was bubbly and cheerful.

Corinne would say that White Eloise was similar to the young girl in the photo, so White Eloise must have been the real daughter of the royal pâtissier.

Having that thought in mind, Corinne peered at the photo, her eyes focused on the young girl with a beaming smile. An odd feeling began to bubble in her mind as her hand reached out for the photo in order to take a closer look.

Being too focused on the picture in front of her, Corinne accidentally knocked over a pile of books.

'Shoot!' Corinne thought.

As soon as her elbow made contact with the stack of journals, Corinne's fast reflexes kicked in. Corinne dove in with both her arms outstretched, all the books that were raining down from the desk fell into her arms.

A breath of relief left Corinne's lips as her eyes swiped towards the door that was still closed. Thankfully, nobody came to give her a surprise attack.

After placing the books back to where they were on the desk, something that was sticking out from the pages of a journal caught her eyes.

Corinne pulled it out, it was another photo.

When Corinne's eyes fell upon the picture in her hand, she was stunned. Her free hand grabbed the framed photo from the desk, holding it next to the piece of picture.

The Eloise in the picture she found in the journal was the complete opposite of the Eloise in the photo frame.

Unlike the Eloise that was radiant with joy, this Eloise looked more composed and quieter, with a small smile on her face, and she looked more like... Black Eloise.

Looking at the two photos in her hand, Corinne couldn't help but furrow her brows and pout. She thought that she was sprinting on the path of revealing who was the real Eloise and reality hit her like a brick wall.

Corinne set down both photos and picked up the journal where the photo was in earlier.

Her eyes lit up when she saw the content of the journal. It was the royal pâtissier's diary!

XX Day XX Month

Today I needed to make rounds at the cafes in the Kingdom, unlike previous days, my little Eloise was with me.

My heart felt the warmest when she looked at me with her big, round eyes, saying how she wanted to be just like me when she grows up.

XX Day XX Month

I was making pastries in the kitchen today and my little Eloise came in saying that she wanted to make sweet things too.

I laughed when I saw how her face was covered in flour, I love my little daughter.

Corinne flipped through the diary of the royal pâtissier, he wrote about his daily life and heart-warming moments with little Eloise.

Corinne skimmed and scanned through those pages because she was a fast reader, until she saw this...

XX Day XX Month

My little Eloise is engaged to the prince, and I am happy for her. Once upon a time she was an infant. Now, she is getting married.

Frowning, Corinne was shocked. Eloise is the prince's fiancée?

Corinne couldn't believe what she just discovered. From their brief meeting earlier in the day, the prince didn't seem like he loved her. Who knew what was really going on in the royal family?

XX Day XX Month

Eloise is ill. She is bedridden. Why did this happen to my poor baby?

XX Day XX Month

I followed the advice of the doctor and sent Eloise back to my hometown to recuperate, hoping that her health will recover.

As though to signal that her time in the chamber was up, the same clicking footsteps could be heard once again.

Hearing the sound of the clicking high heels getting closer to the chamber, Corinne immediately placed everything back and restored them to how they were before.

Her eyes swept over the ceiling, then to the window. The sky was getting dark, she should be getting back to the cafe before the monsters started to roam the streets.

Corinne wasn't afraid of getting into combat with the monsters, but it was better to be safe than sorry. It only took her a split second to make her decision.

When the tall maid opened the door and entered the chamber, she looked around and her eyes fell upon the desk. She paused briefly before she exited the room.

By then, Corinne was already running back to the cafe.

CHAPTER 13

Corinne grinned all the way back to the cafe. But when she burst through the door, her smile turned into shock. Her eyelids fluttered like mad.

Lying in a pool of blood, Perry lay dead with a look of terror on his face, as though he saw something frightening before his life was taken. His rib cage was torn open, and his heart was gone.

Quinn was lying on a table, unconscious.

"What happened?" Claire asked, panting as she came in through the front door.

Corinne shook her head, "I have no idea, I also just came back."

Danny turned green, covering his mouth, and ran to the corner, retching.

Mia had tears in her eyes, her whole body was trembling, "Is he...?"

"He's dead," Ava said, her lips became a firm thin line.

Hearing that, Corinne turned pale, "Quinn!"

When she noticed that Quinn was still breathing, the breath that she didn't even realize she was holding escaped her lips.

"I... think Quinn is sleeping," Claire said, her eyes twitching.

An odd expression flashed through everyone's face.

"Let's just try to wake him up for now," Ava said.

When Quinn woke up, he rubbed his eyes, "What...?"

Out of the corner of his eyes, he saw blood and Perry's dead body. He became ghastly pale, tears pooled in his eyes as both his hands flew up to his mouth.

He was frightened by the terrible sight revealed in front of him.

"I... I don't know what happened. I re-really have no idea," Quinn was shaking, stuttering with his words.

"It's okay, take a deep breath," Corinne said, and gave Quinn a reassuring smile.

Quinn did as he was told, and that seemed to have calmed him down.

Brows furrowed, Quinn recalled what happened, "I remember Perry and I were having snacks while waiting for you guys, when I finished mine, I suddenly felt drowsy..."

That was when Corinne noticed a pot of tea and a basket of muffins sitting on the table.

"Was the food drugged?" Ava asked.

Danny who was reaching out for muffin, instantly pulled his arm back.

"I think the food should be safe to eat," Claire pointed out as she examined a muffin.

"I agree," Corinne nodded, "I'm not sure if you guys noticed this, I believe the food Butler Owen served can relieve fatigue."

Last night, when Corinne *devoured* as much food as she could, she noticed an energy flowing into her body, replenishing her from the exhaustion, which was why she had a sound sleep and felt energized this morning.

"If that is the case, did the murderer kill Perry in his sleep?" Mia asked. She still looked frightened, but she was calmer than earlier.

"Whoever did that must be extremely powerful," Corinne pointed out.

The others looked at Corinne, waiting for her to continue.

"Perry was killed in a single blow," Corinne stood up, giving herself a bit of distance.

Her hand outstretched as she tried to mimic the murderer's move. Her hand formed a claw-like hand sign, then in a swift and speedy movement, she hit the wall behind her and clawed out a piece of the fruit cake wall.

Danny gasped and rushed over to see the wall. Danny felt the wall for a bit before he punched the wall.

"Ow!" Danny cried out, looking at the redness that began to form on his hand.

Ava and Mia exchanged a glance, both shocked by how strong Corinne was even with only her bare hands.

Following Corinne, Claire looked around the cafe.

"Corinne is right, there are no signs of struggle," Claire said, signaling to the muffins and tea pot that were safely sitting on top of the table.

"Maybe the reason that Perry did not struggle is because he didn't have time to do that," Ava pointed out.

Corinne couldn't help but nod at what Ava said. The murderer practically attacked Perry with only one move. Perry would have woken up due to the extreme pain, but he could only watch in horror as the murderer ripped his heart out.

Danny looked at the hole on the wall, rubbing his chin. He didn't want to waste the earnings from their daily quota to repair it.

His eyes lit up when he noticed a painting hanging on the wall behind the cash register.

Danny just finished moving the painting and covered the hole when an odd feeling came up. That was when something clicked in his mind, and he dashed back to the tables and chairs.

"Guys!" Danny cried.

When Corinne and the others went over, they saw the tables and chairs that they upgraded went back to how they were before.

"The kitchen!" Danny cried and stormed towards the kitchen.

"How could this have happened? I thought only the manager had access to the cash register..."

"It must have been the murderer..." Corinne said, lips pursed.

Quinn already went over to the cash register.

"I checked the history; someone downgraded the tables and chairs set. But it doesn't have any record of the one who did it," Quinn said.

"The kitchen is safe!" Danny came back running.

Fortunately, they had decided to upgrade the kitchen. Now, meals only needed to be prepared in the kitchen by placing ingredients into cooking appliances, rather than having to prepare them from scratch. The appliances would do all the cooking, so Danny just needed to follow the sequence and press different buttons on the appliances in the correct order to make a dish.

Feeling relieved that at least the kitchen did not get downgraded, Corinne looked at Danny; with Perry dead, Danny was the only chef left.

Danny looked up and flinched upon seeing Corinne's serious expression, he gulped, "Wh-why are you looking at me like that?"

Just like Danny, the others turned to face Corinne.

"Danny is the only chef left," Corinne stated.

Hearing what Corinne said, the others realized how important this was.

With how everyone was restricted to their own particular role at the cafe, and now that Perry was dead, if Danny died also… then nobody could make food for the monsters that came in.

Everyone went silent, and their expressions were heavy.

After a few minutes, they went back to the wooden table. The wooden table had become a meeting area for them.

Ava was the first to speak, "Okay guys, I think, from now on, Quinn, Danny, and Corinne, it is better that the three of you aren't alone."

Quinn and Danny nodded, Corinne nodded as well, but she thought that if needed, she would still go to the palace alone.

"I know, this is a bit late to discuss, but, at this point, I see no harm in being open since we are working together, agree?" Ava continued, "I'll go first."

Ava understood that what she asked had everyone's privacy involved, so to show her sincerity, she decided to be the first to reveal what she had up her sleeve.

"I'm a karate black belt, and these are the items I have," Ava placed a couple of talismans on the table.

Seeing the talismans Ava pulled out peaked Corinne's interests.

"These are lightning bolt talismans, highly effective against ghosts, but not towards monsters. So, I don't think these will be useful at this station," Ava stated.

Corinne stared at the talismans, the symbols and runes were different, but she was a talisman master, she could feel the energy coming from the talismans.

They were only low-level talismans, not as powerful as lightning tempest talisman; however, they were enough to cause some damage to low-ranking spirits.

"These cost me quite a bit of traveller's points, I suggest that you guys get some if you have points to spare. The other thing I have is this," Ava said, taking off her glasses.

"These are *truth glasses*, they are good against illusions." Ava stated, before she gave Mia a look.

"Mine is this." Mia extended her hand with her palm facing up. There was a circle drawn on her hand, just like a tattoo.

Then a crystal ball appeared, floating above her hand.

"Whenever I arrive at a station, it will start to countdown. Once 24 hours have passed, I get to request for a hint to a question, then it will go into cool down for 12 hours," Mia explained.

"Does it always float like this?" Corinne asked, curious.

"Huh?" Mia blinked, then she nodded, "If I want it to, yes."

Mia threw the crystal ball out, then with a flick of her hand, it flew right back to her like a boomerang.

"Is it hard? Will it break easily?" Corinne continued with her questions.

"Umm..." Mia glanced at her sister; Ava nodded.

"No, it is as hard as a diamond," Mia said.

Corinne crossed her arms, looking extremely interested in that glass ball.

"This could make a really good weapon, have you tried hitting monsters or ghosts with it?" Corinne said, her eyes trained on the crystal ball.

Mia gaped, "...Wha-?"

Ava's eyes lit up, "Mia! That's a great idea! You should do that next time."

Mia could only nod, surprised by Corinne's random thinking. But, come to think of it, that wasn't a bad idea at all. With that in mind, Mia's eyes were beaming just like Ava's.

When it was his turn, Quinn gave his signature shy smile and pink tinted cheeks. Looking at the exact same face as Prince Florian, showing that sort of adorable expression, Corinne couldn't stop her heart from fluttering.

Quinn showed them the gem bangle he had on his wrist, "I have a protection item."

Claire's heart dropped and her eyes narrowed in disbelief when she saw Quinn's eyes start to become glassy as tears began to well up in them.

Her eyes met with Ava's and they both had the same thought, *'here we go again, Quinn's show time'.*

"I'm so sorry that I couldn't be of much help, I'm weak and I don't even have many items that could be useful to you guys..." Quinn mumbled and sobbed.

Claire and Ava exchanged glances as Corinne, Mia, and Danny instantly went over to comfort Quinn.

Claire fake coughed, pulling Corinne back to her seat; she had no idea if Quinn was doing this on purpose or not, but whenever the others comforted him, he would throw himself into Corinne's arms and sob.

"As for me, I think it will be easier to show you guys." Claire said as she patted the pocket on her jacket.

Bellina poked out from the pocket, jumping down to the table.

"This is Bellina," Claire introduced, "She's my little princess doll."

Ava's jaw dropped, shocked to see the princess doll that was blinking at them, "Is this... a summoning item?"

Claire merely gave her a smile as a respond.

Ava could feel her heartbeat race, she was already stunned when she saw Corinne pulled out a sword and slashed those monsters like they were nothing, now Claire had a life summoning item?

With only one look, Ava knew that Bellina wasn't a joke, she could feel the intensity coming from the doll. Did all high rank travellers befriend high rankers?

Corinne and Claire did not know that Ava already misunderstood and thought they were high level travellers.

"I only have these," Danny said.

Thump

Everyone's eyes fell upon the small mound in front of them.

The others looked at the pile he dumped on the table and looked at him with narrowed gazes.

Only? Have these?

They wished they could say it casually like him.

Danny was scratching the back of his head and said, "I only got these from the Beginner Big Pack!"

Corinne went from gasp to glare now.

The Beginner Big Pack was so slim on the spin wheel that Corinne could barely see it! Plus, she only got 'Thanks for trying.' She got nothing. Did Danny have max luck or something?

Wait, she thought Danny only got a gift exchange voucher.

Danny noticed Corinne narrowing her eyes at him and said, "I didn't realize I got another spin until the next morning, I swear!"

Everyone went quiet, although they were smiling. Danny sensed a dangerous aura coming from them, especially Corinne. He let out an awkward laugh before he quickly stuffed his items back.

"Well, you guys already saw my sword, I also have some talismans like you guys," Corinne said.

Unlike Danny who revealed that he had a stack of talismans, Corinne only pulled out a few of them. When she saw the shock in Ava's eyes after Danny took out so many talismans and items, she knew that those things must have cost a lot of TP.

Just as she thought, because Ava gave Danny a stern look.

"Danny, next time, you need to be more cautious on who you show your items to; like these talismans, I could see that they were high rank talismans, and they are expensive.

I know that I've said that we should be open since we're working together, but next time be more careful." Ava said.

Danny understood that Ava was giving him honest advice, so he didn't feel offended at all. Instead, he was grateful that Ava was being sincere with him.

"Got it." Danny said.

"Guys, my crystal ball just finished loading!" Mia cried, catching everyone's attention.

CHAPTER 14

Mia placed the crystal ball in the middle of the table, her eyes wandering through her fellow travellers before fixing her gaze on her sister, Ava.

"What should I ask?" Mia asked, biting her lower lip.

She tore her eyes away from Ava, then looked at the others.

"Hmmm..." Danny crossed his arms, trying his best to think.

Corinne looked at him, honestly, they only known each other for a short period of time. However, it was really obvious what sort of person Danny was. Everything he thought showed on his face.

"Danny, you don't have you try so hard, after all you don't want to short-circuit your brain." Corinne said.

Danny tilted his head, "Hm?"

"You look more brawns than brain to me," Corinne said, her lips twitching.

Claire, always the sensitive one, pulled Corinne's sleeve, giving her a disapproving look.

"Corinne don't be rude to Danny. You are definitely more brawn than brain too!" Claire said.

Instead of feeling offended, Danny flashed his pearly whites, scratching the back of his neck.

"You think so? I can say that I'm not the smartest, but I run fast!" Danny grinned.

Seeing Danny like this, Claire couldn't help but feel lucky that the ones who are sitting here weren't evil, if they were, with Danny being so defenseless, people might have killed him and robbed the items he had, especially with him having so many items.

"Anyway, should we ask who killed Perry?" Claire shifted her attention away from Danny and asked.

Getting a hint on who the murderer was might have been beneficial with the current circumstances. The murderer not only killed Perry, but they downgraded the furniture in the cafe as well.

Corinne could only think of one purpose for their doings: to prevent them from meeting their daily quota.

"What about finding out who the real Eloise is?" Ava suggested.

"That might be a good idea, since we need Eloise to cast the spell or something." Claire said.

Hearing that, Corinne leaned forward a little bit, "I actually found some info about the two Lady Eloises."

Corinne told them about what she found in the palace. The conversation between the maids in the corridor, the findings within the chamber of the royal pâtissier.

"Then, do you know who the real Lady Eloise is?" Danny asked.

Corinne shook her head, "I couldn't confirm."

"So, should we ask the crystal ball which one is Lady Eloise?" Mia tilted her head a little to the side.

"What about the location of the wand?" Quinn inputted.

Quinn had been silent throughout the entire discussion. When he made his remark, the chattering discussion among the other travellers suddenly went quiet, as though someone hit pause.

His voice was pleasant, feathery, and calm, like a gentle stream that washed through the chitter-chatter of his fellow travellers.

"Why don't we ask the whereabouts of the wand?" Quinn repeated.

Seeing everyone's eyes were on him, crimson red dusted his cheeks. Head lowered, Quinn shifted his gaze away from the group, he bit his lower lip before he provided his reasons behind asking that question.

"Finding the wand, and sealing the dragon is our main mission," Quinn stated.

He stole a glance at the travellers and saw that they were considering what he said seriously, so he continued.

Quinn turned to Mia and said, "I remembered, the crystal ball will refresh in twelve hours after we ask a question. The next question can be asked before nightfall tomorrow."

Eyes widened in realization, Corinne's eyes lit up, "You're a genius! We can ask about the wand tonight and then, get hints on the murderer tomorrow!"

With that being said, the group surrounded the crystal ball, all eyes were on it.

Mia gulped, looking left and right at Corinne and the others, "Alright... here we go?"

The others nodded, signaling to Mia that she could proceed with throwing a question at the crystal ball.

Eyes shut, Mia took a deep breath. When she opened her eyes, her whole aura changed.

She was calm as her eyes focused on the crystal ball that flew towards her hands, it floated on top of her palm.

Corinne could see that Mia's lips moved as though she was murmuring some sort of incantation, but she couldn't hear anything.

She thought that there would be something flashy, like a magic circle appearing or glittering lights emitted from the crystal ball, so she patiently waited until she saw Mia place the crystal ball back on the wooden table.

Then, the crystal ball went whirr, then whoosh, and a paper came out from it just like a printer.

Corinne: "..."

Mia took the piece of paper, gave it a quick glance before she turned the paper towards them.

[So far and yet so near.]

"So far... and yet so near..." Corinne read it aloud, deep in thought.

Brows furrowed, Danny ran his hands through his hair turning it into a messy nest, frustrated, "What does that mean?"

Claire muttered the sentence a couple of times, her eyes roaming the room as she thought.

Looking out the window, she could see the silhouette of the chocolate fountain statue under the evening sky.

When Corinne went to the castle to do her investigation, Claire went back to the place where they first arrived, which was the town square, to see if there were any clues about the location of the wand.

She was surprised to see the town square was completely fine. There hadn't been any sign of the attack they had experienced the other day, as though it was just a bad dream.

In the frenzy of the dragon trying to capture and devour them, it had knocked down walls and buildings. Claire remembered clearly that the dragon swept its tail against the fountain, destroying the statue, but there was no trace of this discord now in the town square.

It looked completely fine, as though the attack didn't happen at all.

Initially, Claire thought that the whole town had been refreshed, until she spotted a broken window at a nearby cracker-bricked house.

When Claire's eyes fell upon that house with a shattered window, a thought flew into her mind, and she was about to grasp it when Danny showed up.

Her train of thought was disrupted when she saw Danny leap towards the fountain and try to rip the wand that was in the hand of the statue.

Recalling that, Claire couldn't help herself from sending Danny a stunned glance.

Danny was thinking hard about the hint printed on the paper when he saw Claire giving him that expression. He blinked and then flashed a wide grin.

Claire returned his grin with her own smile, but her lips were actually twitching.

"Guys!" Corinne cried, standing up all of a sudden.

Everyone turned towards Corinne as she paced around the cafe.

"So far and yet so near!" She said, her eyes wide and sparkling, "It must be the cafe!"

"What?" Danny blinked, confused.

"We thought that the wand was so far that it was out of reach, but truth is, it is closer than we think." Corinne explained.

Claire instantly caught on, "And the place that is closest to us, is this cafe!"

Hearing that, the rest of the group brightened up.

"Then, what are we waiting for? Let's turn this place upside down!" Ava exclaimed.

Corinne and the others went through every single corner, every accessible place on each floor of the cafe building. The brunette searched in every nook and cranny, but still couldn't find any-thing.

Refusing to give up just like that, Corinne climbed up to the rooftop of the cafe. Her eyes swept through the tiled roof, kneeling down to check underneath the tiles, and carefully searched through it even though chances were slim.

Letting out the breath that stuck in her throat, Corinne stood on the edge of the roof after she couldn't find anything. Her eyes landed on the ornate castle up in the distance. The silhouette of the building was visible even though it was far away, it stood out against the darkening sky.

The sun sank below the horizon, and the sky cooled. The majestic palace made out of various sweets cast a dark shadow on the candy stone road that led to its front gate, making it look like an ancient tomb comprised of sugar and flour.

Her hands went over to the beaded bracelet on her wrist, she couldn't help but feel that the whole search might be nothing but a wild goose chase.

Corinne had always been an optimistic person; however, she had no idea why she felt slightly down all of a sudden. Maybe it was because of the soft breeze that was gently brushing against her skin, or the darkening sky, the atmosphere that surrounded her as she looked far towards the castle.

Sucking in a deep breath, Corinne's fingers ran over the bracelet, the negativity that was bubbling in her head faded away, and her tightening lips curved up into a little smile.

"Corinne! It's getting dark, come back down!"

The brunette looked down and saw her best friend waving at her, calling for her attention, asking her to get back inside.

"Did you find anything?" Ava asked as soon as Corinne entered the cafe.

Everyone was looking at her, their eyes filled with anticipation. As much as Corinne wanted to say that she found something so the others won't feel disappointed, she shook her head.

The others were clearly discouraged since they couldn't find anything either.

Everyone sat on the floor in a circle with the piece of paper that came out of the crystal ball sitting right in the middle.

So far and yet so near.

Corinne was deep in thought, those words kept on repeating in her head. She was sure that it meant the wand was close to their reach.

Her mind was racing, Corinne was so focused in her little world that she wasn't aware of her surroundings until she caught a delicious aroma in the air.

She glanced up and realized that the others were just as engrossed in their own thoughts as her.

That was when Corinne noticed something odd. She stood up, looking around as though she was searching for something.

"What's wrong?" Claire asked.

"Where's Perry?" Corinne said, moving towards the spot where Perry's corpse was.

The dead body was gone, and the floor that was filled with a pool of blood had become spotless. The empty dinner table was now filled with various dishes.

Corinne's stomach growled; the delicious looking food made her mouth water. All the questions and thoughts that were filling up her mind were instantly being thrown out the window as she found herself moving towards the table like a zombie that was attracted to human brains.

Quinn shyly walked up to them, "I just used the cash register to remove all the dirty things in the cafe, and purchase dinner because..." he gazed out the window, looking at the dark sky, "It is getting late, and we still need to meet the daily quota for tomorrow."

'Dirty things?' Claire raised a brow, *'is he talking about Perry?'*

Quinn turned beet red again when everyone stared at him. "I'm sorry, did I do something wrong?"

Claire: "..."

'Here we go again...' she thought.

'It is Quinn's showtime,' Ava thought.

Both Claire and Ava exchanged a glance as they sighed.

"I... I just thought that it is getting late and..." Quinn sobbed.

It was clearly an act, but the problem is, Corinne and the other two naive ones bought it!

Claire watched by the sidelines as Quinn continued to sob in Corinne's arms, it must have been because of his looks. He was a divine beauty, but Claire just had the urge to punch him in the face whenever he started his *acting show*.

Ava cleared her throat, "Why don't we dig in and head to bed early?"

CHAPTER 15

In the sky, the last few light rays faded away. All the lights were extinguished throughout the kingdom, and Ava could hear the monsters howling in the distance. Just like the night before at nightfall, the monsters took over the streets.

Ava was lying in her bed, thinking about all the events that happened ever since she arrived at this station. She and her sister, Mia, weren't newbie travellers, but when they arrived, the system clearly stated that this was a trial station for new travellers.

It had been explained that their roles for this station were to act as a guidance and provide assistance to new travellers while at the same time completing the missions for this station. In exchange for assisting the new travellers they would get traveller's points; the more newbies survived, the larger the points they got when this station ended.

The odd thing was the only newbie seemed to be Danny. That wouldn't be possible, if Danny were the only new traveller, she and Mia wouldn't get that assistance mission.

What about Corinne and Claire?

Ava thought for only one second before she shook her head, they were strong, and they seemed to have adjusted really well to the situation. They just didn't seem like newbies to her.

Quinn...

Just the thought of Quinn gave her a headache, especially with how he like to put on a *show*.

Ava turned to the other side of the bed, rubbing her temples as a sigh left her rosy lips.

Wait!

What if, Corinne and Claire were actually more senior than her and Mia? And they were the ones that got the assistance missions to help them? That could be possible; after all, she and Mia technically only went through three stations.

Brows furrowed, Ava's fingers that were on her temple went to the bridge of her nose. Ava took in several deep breaths, pushing all the running thoughts away, calming herself and preventing herself from overworking her brain cells.

Ava shut her eyes, she should stop thinking about this and actually focus on the important stuff like the main mission of this station. She felt like they hadn't made any progress at all, and the thought of that was adding to her stress level.

She had gone through three stations, yet she still wasn't used to this. The more Ava tried to force herself to sleep, the more awake she was. Ava sighed, and began to count numbers, hoping that she would eventually fall asleep.

She was super envious of anyone that was able to get a sound sleep.

There were actually several people that were laid-back and care-free. For one, Danny.

The energetic, airhead Danny. The minute he made contact with his bed, he was sound asleep. If someone asked him, was he not concerned or scared about not completing the missions, Danny would probably grin, flashing his pearly whites, and say something like, that wasn't even on his mind. Plus, he was confident in the skills of the others, all he wanted was to stay close to strong travellers and wing it all the way through.

Corinne was the other one that did not have any difficulty falling asleep.

She might look like she was gullible or carefree and gave off vibes like Danny. But she actually knew what she was doing, and always had a clear plan in her head, which was the reason why when she got to bed, she was certain on what she needed to do the next day.

Ding Ling Ling

Corinne could hear the sound of bells ringing as the sign turned to open.

She stood by the door like a pole, she could feel the heavy stomps from the monsters that were coming into the cafe.

Hmm?

Brows knitted together, Corinne peered her eyes at the group of monsters that were seated. Her eyes swept through each and every one of them, when her suspicion was confirmed, she instinctively glanced towards Claire.

Their gazes locked, and Corinne could see her lips turned into a firm thin line. With just one glance, Corinne knew that Claire noticed it as well.

The numbers of higher rank monsters had increased. Yesterday, most of their *customers* were lower rank monsters.

The higher rank monsters were larger, more menacing, even their equips and weapons were higher in quality than the other monsters that only held a wooden bat or branch.

Both Claire and Mia moved from table to table to take the orders from the monsters who were seated.

The timer above the monsters' heads that became yellow when they were waiting for the waitresses, reset back to green when their orders were taken, and started counting down again.

Corinne cursed under her breath, if the murderer did not downgrade their furniture, the waiting time of the monsters would have been prolonged, and their patience would be increased.

Corinne looked towards the window where the completed dishes will be put out, then at the timer again.

With only Danny in the kitchen, he was in a flurry preparing the meals. The small notepad papers with the orders written on them, flooded the kitchen. The papers floated in the air in front of him, lining up in the order that the orders were taken.

She knew the swamp of orders put immense pressure on Danny, especially since he was the only chef here, and knew that messing up would cause trouble for the others.

Looking up, Danny could see what was going on outside through the little window on the kitchen door. Seeing how hard the others were working, Danny gritted his teeth, eyes focused on the task at hand.

Thankfully, they upgraded the kitchen appliances; with Perry gone, the upgrade actually helped a lot.

Everyone was working hard at the café, Claire moved over to the window to pick up the dishes that were ready. For a minute there she was slightly worried that something might have happened after the difficulty increased today.

When Claire saw the cake on the plate, she flinched.

It was a perfect white chocolate and cake pop ice-cream dessert. It was nicely baked, everything was well done, except this wasn't the order.

The customer wanted dark chocolate.

Claire whipped her head over her shoulder, her eyes went wide when she saw the timer for that monster went from yellow to red and was dangerously close to running out of time.

She bit her lower lip, Danny wouldn't have time to remake this, even if he did, it will slow the other orders down.

Corinne, who was just standing by the door and had been observing the entire café, immediately noticed that something was wrong. Her eyes went over to the timer that was previously red and now it was shaking furiously like it was about to explode.

Even though it was the wrong order, Claire was about to just go ahead and serve it anyway when she halted in place, surprised to see that Quinn went over to the monster.

Seeing that Quinn stepped close to the monster that was about to go berserk any second, Corinne wanted to go over only to realize that she was stuck in her post.

The timer on top of the monster's head turned into a speech bubble indicating that Quinn and the monster were in a conversation.

Corinne watched as Quinn said something, and bowed a little, Quinn was probably apologizing to the monster. Then, he said something which the monster responded to with a shake of its head.

Then, Quinn proceeded to talk to the monster, and the monster banged the table with its fist. Corinne saw Quinn turned pale, his hands were trembling slightly, if Corinne didn't have such good eyesight, she would not have noticed it.

Quinn still put on a polite smile, pulling out something that looked a lot like a discount voucher. The monster roared, standing up all of a sudden, knocking over the chair.

The speech bubble popped.

The monster growled loudly, flipping the table causing a loud crash. Quinn froze in place, the others watched in horror as the monster went berserk.

Corinne leaped forward, pulling out her sword. A soft golden light enveloped her sword, as she charged towards the monster's direction. At the speed of lightning, Corinne grabbed Quinn by his arm and swung him to the other side while lifting up the sword to block the claw that was coming her way.

Clang!

The monster's claw clashed with the sword.

Corinne's feet pressed firmly on the floor, the monster was strong, luckily Corinne wasn't weak either.

Corinne pressed her weight a little bit further before she sprung back, the monster's claw hit the ground, resulting in cracks forming on the floor.

Corinne backflipped, swinging her sword forward, and with a swift twirl of her wrist, she charged up the energy of the sword and slashed at the monster.

The golden energy wave stormed towards the monster, slicing it into half. The monster shattered like broken glass, and diminished into thin air, a bag of coins dropped to the floor in a clinking sound.

Corinne raised a brow, her sword minimized and turned back into a pendant, attaching itself back to the golden chain around her neck.

Throughout the entire fight, the other monsters didn't even look in her direction, they just sat there and continued to eat their food as though they were in their own little world or a separate dimension.

The others were stunned by the turn of events, while Corinne picked up the pouch filled with coins and tossed it to Quinn.

"Guys! Let's do this!" Corinne said, her face beaming with a huge smile.

Claire was the first to move, she continued to serve the orders. The others worked on their tasks respectively, more smoothly this time.

They silently agreed on ignoring the extra complex orders that would disrupt their momentum and proceed with the other orders. The higher the rank of the monsters, the more complicated their orders were and the less patient they were.

When Corinne realized that killing the monsters would practically rob them blind, and their money will be added to the quota, she was shaking in excitement.

Whenever a monster went crazy, she would dash forward and kill it without a single blink.

Claire was a bit concerned when she saw how Corinne's eyes sparkled as she held the coin bag in her hand, before grinning widely and running towards Quinn to hand it over to him.

Their cafe was practically a gangster inn, customers came in to eat something delicious, but they would be paying with their lives...

Seeing how excited Corinne was, Claire couldn't help but voice out, "Don't overwork yourself, don't forget about the closing."

Corinne stuck out her tongue playfully and scratched the back of her head, she really did forget about closing time. She still needed to deal with the monsters that couldn't get in during operating hours.

After Claire's warning, Corinne refrained from using too much of her energy. So instead of charging in with her sword, she turned to her talismans. She would eliminate the monsters using flame wave talismans which were more effective against beasts than the lightning talismans that were mainly used against ghost.

Ding Ling Ling

It was closing time.

Danny came out, his face paled with exhaustion; the others looked slightly better than him.

Danny plopped down on an empty table with a pout and started whining, "We must upgrade the kitchen again!"

Seeing that Corinne was by the window peering out, Danny dragged his tired body up and joined the others. When he saw the huge crowd of monsters out there, he gulped.

At merely the sight of the monsters, he could already feel the terror. To fight against the monsters that were so big that they couldn't see their feet, so many they were too numerous to count, and each had such terrifying presence, was truly a Herculean task.

Danny couldn't imagine what he would do if he got the role of security. It would have been suicide for him to try to slaughter those monsters. Danny was proud of himself for making the decision to stay close to Corinne and the others, they were definitely strong.

Corinne stretched, pulling her weapons, and stepped out from the cafe into the sea of monsters.

Noticing Corinne's presence, all the monsters simultaneously turned towards the brunette with intimidating glances.

Without wasting a single second, Corinne whipped out her talismans, sending a wave of flames towards the monsters.

CHAPTER 16

"Poor Lady Eloise...not only did the royal pâtissier pass away, but she had to go through that tragic thunderstorm. Thankfully, even though the ship sunk, Lady Eloise survived..."

Those words replayed in Corinne's mind as she once again stepped foot into the castle.

Sunken ship...

Corinne was standing at the same spot in the corner of the corridor, looking through the vase of lollipop flowers towards the chamber of the former royal pâtissier, recalling the scene from yesterday.

When the two maids hurried off, she remembered one of the maids was mumbling something. But she did not catch the words clearly because she was in a hurry to enter the chamber.

Corinne shut her eyes tightly when the maid walked away, what did she say?

She remembered the maid was holding a pail, a cloth was hanging on the bucket.

"I... room... ship..."

Corinne's eyes flew open.

"I need to clean up the things they managed to save from the ship."

That was what the maid said when she was moving the other way.

As Corinne was about to walk towards the direction where the maid had disappeared to, a shadowy figure emerged from behind her. When she looked up, she saw a maid in a uniform that was split in the colors of white and black. Her eyes grew wide at the sight.

The last time she saw this maid, she had a serious expression on her face and a stern set to her mouth. Now though, she had a wide smile plastered on her cake-white face. Her lips stretched so far that they made her look like she was that slit-mouth ghost from the stories.

"May I know what you are doing here?"

Unlike her impassive vibe, her voice came out in a high pitch, sounding just like a squeaky toy.

Corinne's eyes went over to the name tag pinned on her lace apron.

"Olivia," Corinne said.

She turned towards the maid's direction, looking at her face to face with a bright smile of her own, showing the medal she'd gotten from the prince.

"Olivia," Corinne repeated, "now that you are here, take me to the room where they keep the things from the ship."

Corinne was just wondering how she was going to find the correct room where they stored those items when *Olivia* appeared. It was certainly perfect timing!

Olivia was giving off an intense, menacing vibe. She thought Corinne would be horrified, but much to her surprise, the brunette was smiling widely, and her eyes were twinkling as she played with the medal that she gotten from the prince.

Olivia gritted her teeth, even though this girl had gotten that medal which give her access to freely enter the castle grounds, that didn't mean she could just roam around the palace as if it was her home.

Before Olivia could show Corinne who's boss and whip out her sharp long nails, a small hand encircled her wrists and then, to her surprise, the grip tightened like a heavy chain was being clasped on her.

"Olivia, come on! I think it is this way!"

Olivia almost tripped over her feet when the brunette with herculean strength pulled her along as she pointed to a certain direction and began moving over speedily.

Olivia: "..."

"Olivia, which room is it?" Corinne paused, tilting her head as she asked.

Olivia: "..."

Olivia glanced down to where Corinne's hand was, she was holding her hand now. Corinne swayed Olivia's hand, asking in a whiny voice and even giving her the puppy dog eyes.

Olivia screamed internally, feeling so disgusted. *'Please don't act like we're buddies!'* she thought.

Corinne was laughing her head off inside, but her expression remained cute, she was doing it on purpose to annoy Olivia and seeing Olivia's reaction just make everything so much more fun.

Even if Olivia went on a rampage, Corinne was confident that she would be able to take her down, and if she couldn't fight her, there was the option of fleeing.

"Oh! We're here, thanks Olivia. You're awesome," Corinne purposely made her voice honey-sweet, just to annoy Olivia.

"I still have things to tend to, I'll be off then," Olivia said.

Her words came out quickly and she ran off at the speed of lightning.

Corinne watched as she sped off, bent over, and laughed.

The broken window and the scene of the town square was stuck in Claire's mind.

When Corinne left for the palace, Claire headed straight for the town. She still thought that she was missing something important.

The chocolate fountain with the statue still stood in the middle of the town square in perfect condition. When Claire got close to it, she knelt down to check on a spot.

On the edge of the fountain where it was decorated with flower shaped candies that looked like jewels, Claire literally peeled one off. The flower candy jewel was sitting in her pocket.

Seeing the hole she created, Claire felt like her suspicion might have been true. When she stood up, she spotted something missing from the statue.

The chocolate statue of the royal pâtissier had been holding a wand, but now the wand was gone. Claire recalled the person that was with her when she saw it last was Danny. She remembered how Danny was trying to rip out the chocolate wand from the statue. She did not expect him to *actually* take it.

After she saw the damage she caused was not restored, the idea of the place getting refreshed anew was cancelled off from her list of suspicions.

If the damaged properties did not get magically fixed somehow, then what about the ruckus caused by the dragon that attacked them when they first arrived?

Claire could remember vividly how the dragon destroyed the houses near the fountain, even the chocolate statue was wrecked. She recalled that her attacks did not cause any harm to the beast, not to mention how odd it was that Corinne's high damage skills didn't even manage to scratch the dragon.

A thought vaguely flashed through Claire's mind as she tried to put all the puzzle pieces together.

With all of the thoughts running through her head, Claire did not realize that she had walked back to the cafe.

'I must have walked further than I thought, I'm already back,' Claire thought.

Before she picked up her pace and ran up to the door, her steps were halted as she looked around her. She couldn't shake away these odd feelings she had been getting. Claire thought that she might have been overly sensitive until she saw something that made her heart fall.

At that moment, all the questions in her head were gone, and the missing puzzle piece was found.

Claire immediately pulled her hand away from the doorknob, stepping away from the cafe.

Clang!

The people in the cafe looked towards the entrance, but they saw nothing.

When Claire accidentally kicked the cafe outdoor decoration, her eyes went wide when she saw the lollipop decoration. As much as she was surprised by it, she immediately came back to her senses and hid herself at the other side of the house that was next to the cafe.

Claire held her breath, she could not believe what she just saw and discovered. She could feel her top sticking to her back due to the cold sweat that layered her skin.

There was another cafe that looked like a replica of theirs!

That was why Claire had this odd feeling lingering within her when she stepped foot into this area: because this part of the kingdom wasn't where she had been staying. It was so creepy that they looked exactly the same with only tiny differences that one could hardly notice.

If Claire had not kicked the lollipop decoration by accident she wouldn't have noticed. The lollipop at their cafe was red, here it was pink.

What shocked Claire the most wasn't the replica cafe, but the person she saw in the cafe.

Perry was standing right there!

The Perry that was supposed to be dead!

That was not all, the travellers that she thought were eaten or killed by the dragon... they were all there.

The breath that was caught in Claire's throat escaped her lips, the fog in her head cleared up and she got the answer to the questions that bothered her all this time.

Illusion!

This explained why the damaged properties looked fine and why the town square looked like the dragon had not even been there.

The other travellers that were in the square might have run here instead of to the other cafe.

Now that Claire answered one question, new ones popped up.

Why is Perry alive?

Why would the dragon cast illusion against them?

Was the dragon they saw that day even real, or was it also an illusion?

With all these questions in her mind, Claire was about to head back to the cafe when she saw a white carriage pull up in front of the coffee shop.

Claire pulled back and hid herself in the shadows, her eyes growing wide when she saw who came down from the carriage and headed towards the cafe.

What first came to sight was a pair of white heels. Then, it was a puffy, white lace dress.

It was White Eloise!

'What is she doing here?' Claire thought, *'if there is a way for me to get closer without anyone noticing...'*

Claire wanted to sneak over, but the carriage was still parked in front of the cafe and the coachman was standing right there. Extremely troubled, Claire did not want to give up on the chance to find out what was going on.

Just then, Claire felt a pat on her calf.

She looked down and saw Bellina.

"Bellina? What are you doing here? I thought I asked you to guard Danny," Claire asked in a low voice to prevent anyone from noticing their presence.

After realizing that they only had one chef left, Claire had asked Bellina to secretly protect Danny. They couldn't afford to lose another chef, especially since they weren't replaceable. If they lost someone at crucial roles, the café's daily operations will be interrupted.

Bellina made a couple of gestures, trying to tell Claire why she was here.

Apparently, Danny did not give up on searching the cafe. He told the others who were there that his instincts told him that the wand was definitely there somewhere in the cafe, and he would not give up until he found it.

Bellina saw that the others weren't planning on leaving the cafe, so she came to get Claire because it was getting late.

Seeing that Bellina was here, Claire's eyes brightened up.

Inside the cafe.

"Lady Eloise!"

The people that were casually sitting around, immediately stood up when they saw who was making an appearance at the cafe.

Bellina, who was hiding in a window box planter, peeped through the glass. Claire linked her senses with Bellina, hence, she was watching everything through Bellina's eyes.

White Eloise stood there with her snow-colored lace parasol, her lips were down-turned, her eyes were sharp as she swept through the travellers there.

Unlike the naive, bubbly, and cheerful expressions she portrayed when Claire first saw her, her whole presence now was the complete opposite, she looked intimidating.

Claire watched as White Eloise went over to a chair. White Owen was quick to pull out a duster, and after he dusted the chair, he placed a handkerchief on it before White Eloise sat down.

"Well?" White Eloise said.

Her eyes landed on the group of travellers, they all visibly stiffened, standing up straight and lining up in front of the woman as though she was their commanding officer, and they were soldiers.

The travellers quickly glanced at each other, silently debating on who should be the one to speak up. They didn't get to continue with their telepathic conversation for long, because White Eloise quickly lost any sort of patience she had.

Her heels clicked against the floor, creating a click-clack sound. The veins on her forehead were bulging and easily visible; even Claire, who was watching everything through Bellina's eyes, could feel the frustration that came from the white-dressed lady.

Without further delay, Claire saw *Perry* step forward from the line.

"Perry was eliminated, and we manage to downgrade Black Eloise's Cafe equipment. The staff there must have struggled to meet their quota with one employee less and their equipment being downgraded," *Perry* said.

White Eloise, who now seemed disinterested and was playing with her lace fan, seemed to have perked up after hearing that. Her eyes went over to *Perry*.

When White Eloise looked at him, he lifted his hand and a soft light glowed from the ring on his finger. Then *Perry* turned into a different young man right before Claire's eyes. That must be his real form. The ring must have been one of the traveller's items and he used it to disguise himself as Perry.

As a smirk spread across her face, White Eloise opened her fan. Her features were lovely but the look in her eyes and the curve of her lips made her look terrifying.

"I don't have much time left to seal the dragon. Finding the wand is my top priority, but I also don't want Black Eloise to get ahead of me. If I can't find it, she can't either, understand?" White Eloise closed her lace fan and stood up swiftly.

"Now, tell me. What are you going to do next?" White Eloise inquired.

A woman who stood beside the young man with the ring stepped out to answer, but before she could, a loud and sharp quacking noise split the air.

Claire's hands flew to her ears as she screamed in her head: *'Bellina! Come back!'*

"Intruder!" The woman cried.

Most of the travellers in the cafe dashed towards the door while some went over to the windows inspecting every corner.

The duck who was quacking as though someone was going to kill it, and it headed straight to the window where Bellina was hiding earlier.

The woman tailed behind it, she pushed open the window, but apart from candy flowers, there wasn't anything there.

"Was it a false alarm?" she muttered, looking at the duck that had gone silent.

Claire hid on top of the abandoned building, keeping an eye on the cafe. Once she was sure she wouldn't be seen, she patted Bellina on the back and gestured for her to climb onto her shoulder. Bellina's small hands then grabbed Claire's shirt.

Taking one last look towards the cafe... no... she should say White Eloise's Cafe now, Claire glanced at the rooftop of another house in front of her, gauging the distance between them.

She turned to Bellina, "Ready?"

Bellina replied to her by nodding her head, her curls bouncing along with the movement.

Claire took a couple of steps back trying to do a run-up.

Bellina suddenly pulled on Claire's top, and Claire felt a sharp, slicing pressure coming her way.

Claire reacted quickly, diving to the side and rolling over. She looked over to where she had been standing moments before, and it was now covered in a flurry of feathers.

Steel feathers.

"Huh? You're quicker than I thought."

The attacker was a young girl who looked to be about the same age as Mia. She had a pair of steel wings attached to her back, and with a swift flick of her hand, the wings spread out wide and a rain of feathers shot towards Claire.

Brows furrowed, Claire clicked her tongue.

"I seriously don't have time for this," Claire mumbled.

When Claire finished with her words, Bellina's head turned huge and gobbled up the feathers that were shot straight at them.

The winged girl was shocked when Claire launched an attack against her, and before she could retaliate in full force, she was surrounded by a silvery thread. It wrapped around her, slowly turning cocooning her. In the next instant, the threads grew thicker and thicker, covering her entirely. She was trapped in the cocoon, completely enveloped by the threads.

Thud!

A soft light shone; the threads faded away as a doll dropped down onto the roof. Unlike the free-flowing Bellina, the winged girl doll was conscious yet unable to move. She was like a caged creature, stuck within a rigid shell that no force could break through.

Claire was about to run and jump to the other roof when she paused, looking over her shoulder at the winged girl doll.

"Don't worry, you'll turn back eventually," Claire said.

At times like this, Claire couldn't help but wish that she could brought Bob with her. Bob, the name might sound plain, however, he was actually a gargoyle. He had mighty strength and a pair of strong wings.

Claire sighed, unfortunately, she was limited to only one doll per station unless she could get points to unlock her traveller inventory.

After that, Claire hurried across the rooftops, heading towards her cafe. She needed to warn the others about what she had discovered. She glanced at the castle from a distance, hoping that everything was going smoothly for Corinne in the palace.

CHAPTER 17

Corinne was in a big trouble.

A minute ago, she was laughing her head off for successfully pranking Olivia. But, after that karma came to bite her. Is that why Claire always warned her to refrain from pranking people?

Here she was, standing in a room... wait, actually this was more like an attic. The attic was filled with bookshelves lining the walls, storage boxes scattered across the floor, and bags piled on top of each other.

Just as Corinne was about to sort through all the belongings, Black Eloise suddenly appeared behind the pile of luggage. Her face was wet with tears, and she was clutching a photo album tightly to her chest.

"My apologies that you have to see me like this." Black Eloise said as she pulled out a dark handkerchief to wipe away the tears.

Corinne glanced at the album that was set down in front of them; her eyes were drawn to the open photo album, and she couldn't help but examine the picture inside.

When Corinne saw the picture, her heart began to pound. It was a photo of Eloise and the royal pâtissier, but the image had blurred due to water damage from when the ship sunk. The picture looked as though it had come straight out of a horror movie.

Corinne studied the photo carefully, looking for any details that might give out clues. What she noticed was that a servant in the background was wearing a maid's uniform that was similar to what the other maids were wearing in the palace. However, her face was obscured, making it impossible for Corinne to see what she looked like.

Corinne flipped through the photo album, going past the first few pages quickly but slowing down as she reached the most recent photos. There, she paused and scrutinized each of them closely.

When Corinne turned over to the page with the photo she had first seen, a thought came into her mind. *'Yes, definitely something that appeared in a scary movie.'* She thought.

She wasn't really too shocked by the photos, the distortion mostly seemed normal to her given how the photos were water damaged. One thing stood out as strange though. That one particular maid was blurred out in every single photo.

Corinne pointed to the photo, facing Black Eloise. "Who's this?"

Black Eloise must have been too caught up in her emotions to notice that she had dropped her handkerchief. Corinne was quick to grab it before it hit the floor and handed it back to the lady in black.

When her hand made contact with Black Eloise's, Corinne flinched.

"Thank you," Black Eloise put away her handkerchief, failing to notice the confusion that had quickly flashed in Corinne's eyes.

"I will be off then." Black Eloise turned around, making her leave.

This only deepened Corinne's suspicion of her. Corinne wasn't going to let her leave just like that, especially when she caught the panic in her eyes.

"Who's that?" Corinne repeated, her hand wrapped around Black Eloise's wrist.

"She was..." Black Eloise paused, her head lowered a moment before she glanced up again; her face turned back to its usual cold and stoic expression.

"She was merely a maid." Black Eloise said, wringing her wrist back by force.

Her eyes narrowed into a glare, she straightened her back as she stood, once again looking steady and confident. It was as though the Black Eloise with glassy eyes and anxiety were merely a figment of Corinne's imagination.

"I should remind you that you have no right to treat me this way. I am the prince's fiancée and the heir to the royal pâtissier. You are merely a security guard working in my cafe, so it is not your job to question me. If you have time to interrogate me, you should spend it to search for the wand instead of lurking around the palace." Black Eloise warned.

Black Eloise had definitely managed to reclaim her calm demeanor.

Corinne could tell that Black Eloise was unhappy with her. She was certain that if she continued to challenge Black Eloise, Black Eloise would not tolerate it. Still, she could feel that Black Eloise had something to hide.

It seemed like Black Eloise was an NPC on their side, maybe even their ally for a time, given that she was the daughter of the royal pâtissier and because she needed them to search for her father's wand, so she could seal the dragon away.

Corinne paused. She was reluctant to press Black Eloise further, for fear of pushing her too far. She couldn't be sure if Black Eloise would give in or if she would lose her patience and treat Corinne like yesterday's trash.

Corinne smiled at Black Eloise, but she didn't look away. Black Eloise stared back at her for so long that Corinne's smile began to ache, and her cheeks grew sore. At last, Black Eloise turned away and left the attic.

When Corinne was sure that Black Eloise wasn't going to come back, she rubbed her sore cheeks while turning back to the photo album. Her eyes landed on the figure that stood behind Eloise, her blurred face in the damaged photo making it looked eerie.

Something inside Corinne told her that identifying this maid was important, and she believed she could figure out the mystery. She had her suspicions, but how could she confirm them?

The sun began to set, painting the sky in hues of orange. The temperature went down, and the breeze that picked up sent shivers down Corinne's spine even though she was wearing a cardigan over her top.

A warm, hearty aroma filled Corinne's nose as she closed the door behind her and stepped over to the dining table in the cafe. When she spotted the food spread out before her, its look and aroma caused her eyes to light up.

She ran to her chair to sit down. As she plunked down on the chair, Corinne noticed the tense atmosphere of the travellers around her who were seated at the dining table, and she turned towards her best friend.

"Claire, what's going on?" Corinne asked.

Claire reached the cafe earlier than Corinne, Quinn returned right after her, whereas the others did not leave the cafe. Claire was surprised that Quinn actually went out alone, considering how timid he seemed to be.

"Look at this," Claire pushed the newspaper that was on the edge of the wooden table towards Corinne.

Corinne could see the headline on the front page of the paper with its giant capital letters: WHO WILL BE THE PRINCE'S BRIDE?

The big bold letters were hard to miss. Underneath the title was a photograph of the two Eloises and their respective butlers. Black Eloise and White Eloise were next to each other, and if a 'vs' was added in between them it would be like one was against the other in battle.

Corinne ignored the words of praise about the prince and the kingdom, instead skipping to the bottom of the page, which stated that whoever sealed the dragon would be the true bride to the prince.

"Where did you find this?" Corinne asked, after she finished the paper.

Claire gestured to Quinn. Quinn flashed his signature shy smile and pink dusted cheeks.

"They were giving them out in front of the palace," Quinn said.

"You went to the palace?" Corinne asked, brow raised.

She thought Quinn would not go alone, since he was very timid. She didn't see him though, she probably missed him since Claire mentioned he came back just after her.

Claire proceeded to tell her side of the story, this explained why they looked so tense.

The things Black Eloise had said to Corinne in the palace left her in confusion, but once she heard Claire's side of the story, the suspicions she had been harbouring were cleared up.

Based on the differences in their clothing, it was clear to Corinne that the two Eloises were enemies. After all, they both wanted to be the prince's bride, and the prince could only have one bride.

Olivia's maid dress was split in to half white and half black, did that meant that she was neutral? Maybe she wasn't on the side of either Eloise, and she was on the prince's side.

The prince did not show who he favored more though. Recalling the brief encounter with the prince, something flashed through Corinne's mind.

Initially, Corinne thought that with a clear mission given to them at this station, the travellers should work together to seal the dragon.

However, after Claire said that she was attacked by steel-winged girl, the thought of cooperating went down the drain and the feeling of disbelief came up. She didn't know that travellers could actually go against each other.

Corinne told them what just ran through her mind, and then Danny who threw out a question about travellers vs travellers.

"Wait, if both Eloises are in opposing factions, does that mean we are on the black faction? Since we are technically *working* under Black Eloise," Danny asked.

Before anyone could answer, Danny continued to bombard everyone with his questions.

He turned to Claire since she had been face-to-face with the white faction.

"Are they really out to get us?" Danny asked.

Claire might have turned the steel-winged girl into a doll, but that was only temporary. Once the spell wore off, she would turn back into a human. Claire suspected that she would not sit back and do nothing.

"Unfortunately, when steel-winged girl turns back, she might be coming after me," Claire said.

"I thought we are all in this together, do travellers go against their own kind?" Danny asked.

Ava took off her glasses and pressed the bridge of her nose, letting out a tired sigh before she answered Danny's questions.

"I honestly did not expect that this was a PK station."

"PK station?"

"PK stands for Player-Killing. Normally at this sort of station, the travellers will be divided to two opposing factions. Whichever faction comes out as the winner, survives the station basically," Ava explained.

So, that's the reason the travellers from the white faction wanted to get rid of them.

However, Ava still didn't get it.

This was supposed to be a station for trial travellers. She knew about PK stations from the posts in the forum, normally they are for more experienced travellers that went through four or five stations.

Did the travel agency system send them here by mistake?

Just the word killing was enough to drain all the blood from Danny and Mia's face.

"Wh-wh-what should we do?" Danny asked, his words stuttering.

He pulled out his stack of talismans, ready to dash to the door.

Claire grabbed him by the arm, "What are you doing?"

"I'm going to stick these all over the café," Danny said, blinking his puppy dog eyes.

Claire's jaw dropped.

Corinne looked at him, stating the obvious, "You do know that those only work on ghosts and spirits... right?"

Danny cursed under his breath and slapped himself on the forehead, "I forgot!"

He grabbed Corinne's hands as though she was his lifeline, tears rolling out his eyes, "Corinne! Can you whack them to outer space with your Hercules strength?"

A guy that's over six feet pleading like a damsel in distress to Corinne who was only five foot four...

And for some reason, looking at his face and hearing his words made Corinne's fist tighten and gave her the urge to hit him on the head.

Before Corinne could take her hands back, a familiar sobbing sound was heard, and Danny was pushed to the side. Quinn whimpered, throwing himself at Corinne.

"I'm so scared..." Quinn sobbed.

Claire rubbed her temple before clearing her throat to gain everyone's attention.

"Even with the Eloises against each other, we cannot confirm that this is a PK station, right? Don't forget..." Claire knocked the table lightly with her fist.

"Our mission is to seal the dragon," Claire stated.

Her voice was velvety like the flowing river, her words were firm. The others calmed down almost immediately after Claire finished her sentence.

Seal the dragon...

Corinne was deep in thought.

Her eyes were on Claire's fist, to be exact, her eyes were on the table.

The wooden table.

Corinne felt like she was catching on to something.

"But we still need to figure out who the real Eloise is right?" Mia asked, feeling unsure.

"We don't even know where the wand is..." Danny said, sitting back down to the chair, looking like a sad puppy.

"Corinne."

Our mission is to seal the dragon...

"Corinne!"

"Huh?" Corinne looked up and realized that all eyes were on her.

"We were discussing whether we should go ahead and ask the crystal ball who the real Eloise is or try asking for the location of the wand again," Claire said.

"I might have an idea on Lady Eloise," Corinne said, and...

She pulled out a thick album?

Claire felt like her head was throbbing again, "Corinne...did you..."

Corinne beamed at her and nodded, then she told them what happened in the attic.

"And you brought it here?" Claire cried.

She knew that she shouldn't have let Corinne roam around on her own, the minute that she let her guard down, Corinne started to steal. The second that she wasn't with her, Corinne was like a dog off its leash and went wild.

She just stole something from the palace.

And it was important to the Eloises.

Now not only did she have the steel-winged girl that was out to get her, Black Eloise would definitely be after Corinne.

"Claire, chill out." Corinne said in a sing-song voice.

Hearing how happy-go-lucky Corinne was, Claire sent her a death glare, her face went red out of rage.

"You!" Claire started, looking like she was about to burst.

Sensing a nagging session, Corinne began to do deep breathing.

"Claire, deep breath. Come on, breathe in... and out..."

Claire mimicked Corinne and after another deep breath out, she calmed down.

While Claire was focused on being angry at Corinne, the others wondered where she kept the album, she didn't seem like she had it with her. It was like she pulled it out from thin air, this was just like something that happened in manga…

Seeing that Claire wasn't angry anymore, Corinne diverted her attention.

"Anyway—" Corinne changed the subject, "I was thinking we could try to find out who this is…"

She pointed to photo with the maid's face being blurred like it was mosaic because it was bad for the eyes.

The others leaned in to get a closer look at the photo when Mia gasped. Her face, that had finally gone back to normal from the killing conversation earlier, became pale once more.

Looking at the frightened Mia, Corinne tried to comfort her, "Yeah, it looks haunted but no worries, there's no ghost here. If she died in the sunken ship, it will be even better. I can try to summon her so we can ask her who the real Eloise is."

Claire brightened up when she heard that. "Oh, that's right! Since she was Eloise's maid that served her and grew up with her back in the royal pâtissier's hometown. She was with the real Eloise all this time!"

The others in the room went wide-eyed, astonished by the exchange.

Did Corinne just mention that she can summon a ghost? Calling someone from the underworld? And Claire just agreed that it was actually a great idea?

"I know right! It is such a good idea," Corinne nodded happily and was also glad that Claire forgot about being angry with her.

Claire lightly flicked Corinne on her forehead, "Don't think that I forgot about your little stealing adventure."

Hearing that, Corinne pouted and went back to studying the photo.

"Then, do we ask the crystal ball where the maid is instead?" Mia asked, her head tilted a little to the side.

CHAPTER 18

With Mia's question, the others dived into another round of discussions.

Corinne's eyes landed on the photos.

What happened in the attic replayed in Corinne's mind, Black Eloise was crying as she looked through the album.

Did she cry because the maid that grew up together with her died in the tragedy at sea?

Then, her words about the wand.

Brows furrowed, Corinne's eyes were sweeping around the cafe. From the chairs they were sitting on, to the counter nearby, then the lights.

Her eyes grew wider as she looked at more things in the building.

The lamps and windows were made from glass candy. The counter was pound cake. The decoration flowers were lollipops or cotton candy.

Everything here was made from sweets.

So far yet so near...

So far... yet so near!

Corinne's eyes fixated on the table in front of her, her grip tightened on the table.

The others finally noticed that something was wrong with the brunette.

"...Corinne?" Claire muttered.

Corinne abruptly glanced up, "So far yet so near!"

The others exchanged a glance before most of them looked at her with guarded expressions. Danny, however, looked at her shiny eyes like she just went madder than the mad hatter.

Corinne cried and was about to sweep all the food off the table when she paused, taking a couple of trips to set the food on another table.

Claire let out a sigh of relief, whispering to the others, "She still cares about the food."

The others turned to Claire, Claire smiled, reassuring them further, "Don't worry, she is still sane."

"..."

The more they got to know the Corinne and Claire duo, the more they felt speechless with their surprising acts.

Once Corinne was done with whatever she was doing, she came back, looking at them with her round and bright eyes.

"So far yet so near!" Corinne repeated, her eyes glinting, a wide smile plastered on her face.

The others faced Claire once again, looking at her with raised brows as if they were asking her *'Are you sure she is sane?'*

"Look! That's the wand!" Corinne shrieked as she flipped the table over, causing a cascade of surprise from everyone.

"Here it is!" Corinne announced, yanking the wand out of the overturned table. "It's the wand, right?" she said, her voice was uncertain because of how the wand looked.

"This is the wand?" Danny asked, taking it into his hand.

The wand was crooked, looking like a branch that was about to snap in half any second.

Corinne glared at the stick that was now in Mia's hand.

"Is that actually the wand that everyone was looking for?" Claire asked, looking at the wa—uh stick.

"But it should be! According to the hint we got from Mia's crystal ball," Corinne said.

Everything was made out of pastries except for the dining table that was under their noses all this time. They ate their meals at the wooden table every day and held their group discussions at the same table.

All this time, they thought that the wand was somewhere in the kingdom, but it was literally right under their noses.

That was what it meant by so far yet so near!

Claire thought that it actually made sense. However, looking at the wand, she couldn't help but feel dubious because the wand that was supposed to seal a dragon that threatened the entire Cakeland Kingdom was literally a wooden stick.

Before Claire could say anything further, her words got stuck in her throat when Danny pulled out a chocolate wand.

Her eyes went wide when she saw that chocolate wand.

That wand looked identical to the one from the chocolate fountain!

The others looked just as surprised as Claire.

Did Danny really rip it right out from the statue of the chocolate fountain?

Danny looked from the chocolate wand in his hand to the wooden stick Corinne found under the table.

"They don't look the same at all, is this really the royal pâtissier's wand?" Danny asked.

Quack...

"Did you guys hear something?" Mia gulped.

Quack! Quack!

Everyone glanced down and saw a yellow duck that was made out of wood standing in front of them, flapping its wooden wings.

The duck stared at Danny, quacking at him furiously. Looking at the duck's beady, little red eyes sent shivers down his spine. Before Danny could jump away from the duck and hide himself behind the counter, the duck suddenly charged towards him.

Quack!

Claire immediately recognized that duck: it was the duck from one of white faction's travellers.

She whipped her head towards Bellina, "Bellina!"

When Claire called for her, the princess doll was already in action. She leaped towards the duck, caging it within her arms and rolling to the other side, distancing it from the travellers.

Claire was about to go over and help Bellina when familiar waves of steel feathers rained in, shooting against them like machine gun fire.

In only a split second, Corinne kicked the edge of the dining table, flipping it back up and firmly holding the leg of the table, using it as a shield. No need to be told, the others instantly hid behind the table.

Following the steel feathers attack was a fireball, it hit the table and the table was quickly lit up by the fire.

"Get back!" Corinne cried.

Corinne was still holding onto the table leg, she swung it, sending it towards the attackers.

The intruders burst through the door and started attacking them. It was about time for Corinne to attack them, too. Talismans spread out in front of her as she prepared to give them a taste of their own medicine, when she heard the other party said.

"Hand over the wand!"

"Give Donald back!"

"..."

Donald? Seriously?

Corinne's eyes went over to the yellow duck that was quacking, flapping it's wings like crazy. The duck chased after Danny after it managed to escape Bellina's clutches. Danny yelped and started running around the cafe.

So, right now, Danny was running away from the yellow du... Donald while Bellina was chasing Donald.

All of a sudden, everyone became silent except for the sounds of the chase fest. The cafe was filled with Danny's cries, the duck's annoying quacks, and Bellina's mary janes tapping on the floor.

Among the people that barged in, Claire immediately spotted the steel-winged girl, and also the rest of the travellers from White Eloise's Cafe.

"It's them," Claire whispered to the others.

Even if Claire did not tell them, the others also knew that they were the travellers from the white faction. The only travellers that were here at this station were them and the travellers with White Eloise.

Claire did expect their arrival because she accidentally woke a sleeping dog, however, she didn't think that it would be so soon.

"Quack! Quack! Quack!"

"Heeeelp!" Danny cried as he ran around the cafe, throwing whatever he picked up along the way at Donald.

Danny wanted to create obstacles for Donald and make it harder for it to chase him, but Donald could see the obstacles coming and easily avoided them. Danny had not thought about how that would also make it harder for Bellina, who was running behind the duck.

Bellina was running on the same path that Donald used since she was chasing the yellow duck, so she had to jump over all the things that Donald dodge. She was still trying to catch up to the duck though.

Bellina's patience ran out and she turned large, knocking away the tables and chairs, which made Quinn turn pale, calculating how much of the cafe proceeds he needed to use to replace those things.

Seeing that Bellina scooped up the duck, the girl from white faction leapt towards the duck. The girl activated her super-speed sneakers, saving the duck.

Bellina got angry and smacked the girl, the girl dodged by using her super-speed. The duck, who managed to get away, continued to chase after Danny.

"Donald! Come back!" the girl cried, trying to chase after the duck to no avail because Bellina was after her now.

The opposing travellers were getting major headaches seeing such fuss breaking up in front of them.

"Give us the wand!" the young man with shapeshifting ring cried.

The young man transformed into a huge, muscular man who wielded a large hammer. He slammed the weapon on the ground and a trail of sharp thorns broke off and headed right at Corinne.

"No!" Corinne screamed back, throwing a flame wave to counter the attack of her opponent.

A fight erupted between Corinne and the shapeshifter, with Corinne pulling out her sword and spreading her talismans out in front of her in a crescent curve, ready to attack.

The ruckus and noises started to get to Ava. Mia could see the veins popping out on her forehead. Her eyes went from Ava's forehead to her knitted brows and finally landed on her tightened fist.

She shivered just thinking about how frightening Ava was when she exploded out of rage. Her eyes went over to the crazy quacking duck that acted a lot like a tireless stubborn goose. It was all its fault!

Without thinking twice, Mia's crystal ball left her hands. In the next second, the crystal ball that was as hard as diamond landed upon the yellow duck.

Everyone froze for a minute.

Danny stopped in his tracks and his eyes fell upon the now squashed duck. He panted, letting out an exhausted breath before his knees gave out and he dropped to the floor right next to the duck.

Looking at the duck, Danny couldn't help but feel aner against the yellow duck for making him run till he was worn out.

Danny cursed the duck under his breath, doing several air punches like he was beating the crap out of Donald.

"Quack..."

Stunned, Danny grabbed a tray that was left on the floor and began slamming it against Donald.

"Qu-"

Seeing that Donald was still alive, Danny slammed a couple more times until it was torn into pieces.

Mia hissed in pain just looking at what Donald had been through.

"Nooo! Donald!" the girl screamed like she just lost the love of her life after Danny brutally murdered the yellow wooden duck.

"Get away from me!" the girl cried at Bellina, whipping out a hand full of buttons from her jacket.

She threw them at Bellina, Bellina tilted her head in confusion, unsure what mere sewing tools could do to her, and she raised her hand to slap them away when the buttons exploded.

They were button bombs.

Bellina let out a cry due to that explosion, when she looked at her palm, she froze.

The bomb did not cause her to lose her hand or anything, but it created an open wound from which white cotton gushed out from her palm like blood.

Bellina blinked, she couldn't process what was happening to her as her hand slowly became flat like a deflating balloon due to cotton loss. Seeing how her hand was, Bellina frowned, she cast a fleeting glance at Claire, then back at her flattened hand as if she couldn't believe that this was her hand.

Bellina, the princess doll that could tear spirits into pieces and devour malicious ghosts like they were nothing.

Bellina, the doll that could kick-ass in a puffy, fluffy dress and a diamond tiara on top of her head was technically... still a child that was afraid of cotton.

Claire who noticed how Bellina was, mumbled, "Oh no..."

Then, she ran towards Bellina.

"It's okay... it's okay, Bellina!" Claire patted Bellina, comforting the princess doll.

Bang!

Bellina plopped down to the floor and Claire's heart dropped. She was bounced up and dropped back down onto Bellina's lap.

"Waaaaah!"

A roaring cry shook the entire cafe.

Glitter began to pour out from Bellina's sapphire gem eyes, she was crying a river.

Trying her absolute hardest to mute out Bellina's powerful destructive cry, Claire hugged Bellina, looking up at the doll saying comforting words.

Corinne gasped, running over to join Claire to calm Bellina down.

"He-hey! Your opponent is me!" the shapeshifter cried.

Corinne looked over her shoulder, rolling her eyes, "If you don't want to be drowned in glitter, you better get the heck out of here!"

The shapeshifting guy stood there, dumbfounded, until he realized that he was knee-deep in a sea of glitter. His heart sank as he glanced up.

In only a split second, the shapeshifting guy joined the comfort Bellina gang.

Bellina continued to cry like there was no tomorrow. The more she cried, the more she shrunk, however, the amount of glitter tears did not decrease at all. Soon, everyone was in a sea of bluish glitter.

CHAPTER 19

The soft rumbling of the carriage came to a halt when it stopped in front of the cafe.

A pair of white heels clicked the ground when White Eloise exited her means of transportation. When she spotted the lady in black that looked identical to her, her lips became a fine thin line.

However, she had more important things to do at this moment than to express her distaste towards Black Eloise.

Under the sound of crying that resembled the roaring thunder, White Eloise gave White Owen a glance and the butler immediately went over to the cafe.

He was just feeling slightly odd as to why the cafe was completely dark when their cafe staff were *visiting* Black Eloise's Cafe.

When White Owen opened the door, blue glitter gushed out from the cafe, hitting everyone outside like a ferocious tidal wave.

Underneath a glittering mountain, a hand shot out and Corinne emerged, crawling out from the blue glitter, her bun became untied as her brown locks fell down to her chest in a soft wave. Corinne spit out the glitter that was in her mouth and gasped for air.

Then, she saw a lock of curly hair sticking out from the glitters. Corinne hurried over, she grabbed the hair and started pulling with all her might.

"Don't worry! I'll save you!" Corinne said.

When the person that was buried under the glitter was dragged out, Corinne flinched.

It was White Eloise.

Her face was beet red, and her glaring eyes were burning with rage.

Without thinking, Corinne pressed her back down into the glitter.

"Milady!" White Owen screamed in horror when he saw what Corinne did, he rushed over as soon as he managed to get out from the pile of glitter.

When White Eloise was freed, Corinne wasn't even sure if she could call her White Eloise anymore. Her white lace dressed was stained by the glitter and was now a shimmering blue, in fact, her entire outfit became the color of the sea.

Looking at the state of her outfit, a piercing scream sliced through the night sky. Corinne who was only a few feet away got a critical hit. White Eloise's scream was even more difficult to bear compared to Bellina's cry.

Black Eloise, on the other hand stood there silently while letting Black Owen dust her dress using a cotton candy duster.

Ignoring the White Eloise that was throwing a tantrum, yes, in Corinne's eyes White Eloise looked just like a spoiled brat right now. Previously White Eloise was still acting all cute and innocent in front of them, now she did not even try to put in the effort to hide her true bratty self.

Was it because they found the wand?

With that question in mind, Corinne went over to check on Bellina.

Bellina was being cradled in Claire's arm, sniffing. When she noticed Corinne, she glanced up with her sapphire gem eyes, her face was stained with glitter. Corinne's heart throbbed in pain, seeing Bellina looked all depressed like that, Corinne ripped out the lollipop flowers by the outdoor windowsill, making them into a bouquet and handed it to Bellina.

Bellina finally had a little smile spread across her small round face. When everyone's heart was melted by how adorable the little princess doll looked, her head turned large revealing her sharp shark-like teeth and took in the entire candy bouquet in one bite.

Letting out a burp, Bellina shrunk back into key-chain size and rest in the pocket of Claire's jacket.

Different from Bellina who was relaxing; the travelers, especially those from the white faction, were tense.

White Eloise stood in front of them and her anger was clearly visible. Once again, the travelers stood in a line facing White Eloise. All of them wore strained expressions, which indicated their anxiety and hopelessness.

"The wand...did you guys get it?" White Eloise crossed her arms, her eyes narrowed at the travelers.

As soon as White Eloise finished with her words, all of them turned towards Danny. Danny froze, he shook his head profusely, hiding the wands behind his back.

Ava stepped forward, shielding Danny behind her and her eyes fixated on White Eloise.

Following the gazes of the travelers, a smirk spread across White Eloise's powdered white face.

"So, he has the wand," White Eloise said.

Her heels clicked on the hard candy road; each click added pressure to Danny as though she was stepping on his heart.

White Eloise stopped at her track, raising her lace fan, "Oh, and Owen; be a dear and get rid of those useless pests."

The travelers turned pale, they remembered vividly what White Eloise and her butler did on the first day they reached the cafe. The traveler was helpless against White Owen.

White Owen removed his glove, "Yes, Lady Eloise."

Shapeshifter guy gritted his teeth, he wasn't going to go down without a fight. Even if chances of surviving were slim, he still wanted to try. He didn't want to die!

A wall of fire suddenly lit up in front of them, creating a wall between them and White Owen.

Looking over to see who cast that flame wall, they saw Corinne with her talismans spread out in front of her.

"Hold it right there!" Corinne said, whipping out a torn black and white photo and held them in between her fingers.

It was the photo of that maid with blurred face.

"What does a mere maid have to do with all of this?" White Eloise said, slapping Corinne's hand away.

Corinne grabbed her hand. The sensation of White Eloise's soft hand made Corinne raised her brow, she shoved the photo at White Eloise.

"Look closely, do you not recognize her at all?" Corinne asked.

White Eloise snatched the photo away from Corinne, "She's just a maid! Why do you-"

White Owen stepped in, taking the photo from White Eloise and apologizing to her for intruding, "If you would stop bringing up the lady's deceased lady-in-waiting, Mary. The lady is still sad over the passing of Mary that grew up together with her since they were children."

Corinne might have been facing in the direction of the butler in white uniform, but her eyes were on White Eloise. White Eloise pursed her lips, slight panic flashed through her eyes so quickly that if Corinne did not pay attention to her, she would have missed it.

"You took my photo album?" Black Eloise asked.

She had been staying silent the entire time until Corinne pulled out the photo. She rushed over, on edge.

Black Eloise's eyes did not leave photo that was still in White Owen's hand.

"Please give me back the photo," Black Eloise said; her lips forming a firm, thin line.

Seeing how Black Eloise was nervous about the photo, White Eloise took the photo back from her butler.

Lips curled up, White Eloise cast Black Eloise a glance before she tore the photo into pieces and everyone who was watching sucked in a breath.

Black Eloise stared at the pieces of torn photos that littered the ground. She couldn't believe what had just happened. She knelt down to pick up the photo pieces and handed them to Black Owen.

Glaring at White Eloise, she said in a low voice, "You! You did this!"

For the first time ever, Corinne could sense real anger coming from Black Eloise.

Black Eloise stood tall with her back straight, both of her hands placed on her abdomen. Her eyes sharp and cold, her lips were a fine thin line. An intimidating aura enveloped Black Eloise as she sent daggers at White Eloise.

At that moment, everyone held on to their breath, they could literally see blocked letters 'vs' flashing in between Black Eloise and White Eloise.

When they thought a fight would erupt between the two Eloises, Black Eloise was the first to open her mouth.

"I did not want to stand against you, I have never thought of taking anything away from you. All I wanted was to bring peace back to the kingdom," Black Eloise said.

White Eloise crossed her arms and responded to those words with a roll of her eyes.

"But now, I've changed my mind," Black Eloise said.

She walked over to Danny, who was still hiding behind Ava.

"Can I have the wand please?" Black Eloise said, her voice was soft and gentle.

Danny looked at her, Black Eloise had a little smile on her face, she looked kind and gentle whereas White Eloise face was beet red due to anger, she was giving them deadly glare.

The moonshine shimmered down on Black Eloise, blanketing her in a holy yet radiance light. However, it gave off an eerie vibe in Danny's eyes.

Danny gripped onto the wands tightly, he looked at Ava who was closest to him. Ava bit her lower lip, then he looked at the others, unsure what to do.

"Wait! Give me the wand!" White Eloise pushed Black Eloise aside.

"No, I'm the real Eloise, give me the wand!" Black Eloise pushed White Eloise back.

All the travelers watched as both Elouises got into a cat fight, their jaws dropped.

Danny looked at them, acting like two girls who were fighting over a limited-edition Prada bag, except he was the bag right now.

"I can't take it anymore!" Danny cried.

Danny whipped out the stick that he found, "Here! Take it!"

The two Elouises immediately stopped what they were doing, White Eloise took the stick.

Her eyes scanned every inch of the stick doubtfully, "This is the wand?"

Not just White Eloise, even Black Eloise was looking at the *branch* speculatively.

Under the pressure of both their gazes, Danny thought for a moment before he took out the wand that he ripped right out from the hands of the chocolate fountain statue.

Compared to the bent and splintery stick that was worn out and seemly unfitting to use, the chocolate wand was as straight as a line and crafted from the finest ingredients found in the entire Cakeland Kingdom and formed by the highly skilled royal chocolatier.

Its finish was detailed engraving, layered with gold dust that shimmered in the moonlight. A bright candy diamond embedded in the wand sparkled at its tip, drawing both Eloise's eyes.

Tossing the stick away, both Eloise started to fight over the chocolate wand.

"Um... I actually took it from the fountain statue," Danny tried to make his input clear, but the two Eloise were too busy to hear him because they were brawling one another for the wand.

Corinne exchanged a glance with Claire, just one look from Claire and she knew that they were thinking the same thing.

Did they really not know which one was the real wand?

Corinne's eyes went over to the wooden stick that was on the ground, she picked it up and examined it closely. That was when she noticed the tiny engraving at the bottom of the stick.

Peering at the engraving, Corinne took out the chocolate medal she got from the prince. The medal had the same engraving on it. It was Cakeland Kingdom's royal emblem!

Corinne was sure that she got the hint right and the stick must be the wand.

Seeing the Kingdom's emblem on it boosted her confidence.

"Then..." Claire said, glancing over at the two Eloise.

"Who is the real Eloise?"

"It's..." Corinne fell silent when the ground beneath her feet began to shake like the earth was shifting. Then, a dark shadow fell over them and Corinne looked up. A dragon was approaching.

Its shape cast a giant shadow that slid over them and filled the entire space. It loomed overhead like a storm cloud filled with lightning. In the next moment, the dragon's head turned, and Corinne saw its yellow eyes fix on her.

"Wh-why is the dragon here?" White Eloise yelled; her eyes wide with horror.

As if to answer White Eloise's question, the dragon snorted, sending a plume of flame from its gaping mouth and painted the ground with light.

"Run!" Corinne screamed and started sprinting away from the dragon.

CHAPTER 20

Corinne ran in full speed, the dragon seemed like it was attached to Corinne as it kept on tailing her.

The dragon roared, a billow of flame filled the air before it was blasted straight at Corinne. She leapt and rolled over to the other side avoiding the fire ball.

At first, everyone broke off in all different directions to escape from the dragon. Danny had the misfortune to trip on a rock and fall on the ground. However, when he caught his breath, and looked up, he realized that the dragon wasn't after him or any of the other travelers.

In fact, the dragon was uninterested in them and was only after Corinne. The others soon noticed this as well and stopped.

"Why is the dragon only chasing me?" Corinne screamed as she ran.

White Eloise and Black Eloise exchanged a glance with their respective butlers before they both started moving towards their own carriages.

"Wait! You guys have to do something!" Ava confronted them.

"Aren't you suppose to seal the dragon?" Mia joined her sister and asked.

Danny was concerned, he shook Claire by the arm, "what should we do? She can't keep on running like that."

The dragon sucked in a breath, they could see the flames accumulating, the fire ball will be a huge one and if Corinne got hit, chances of surviving were close to nothing.

The more critical the situation was, the calmer Claire looked on the outside. Her inner-self was screaming at her to think, fast! Claire's mind was running in full speed and adrenaline ran through the veins of her entire body.

Claire dashed forward, and with all her might she threw that potato light-bulb at Corinne, "Take the potato!"

If Corinne weren't on a dire situation right now, she will be laughing so hard when Claire said that. She ran a couple of steps forward and caught it just in time.

Then, Claire noticed the crooked stick that was still in Corinne's hands. She was confused as to why the dragon was only chasing Corinne until she saw that wand. The dragon wanted to get rid of it.

"Wait, Corinne, the wand!" Claire said, "The dragon is chasing you because of it! Throw it away!"

Hearing what Claire said actually made Corinne tighten her grip around the wand, if the wand was the reason behind the dragon tailing her, that means that the stick was important.

She activated the light-bulb, it flickered a couple of time before a soft light in the color of pale yellow appeared, enveloping Corinne within the barrier.

The dragon roared, and an enormous fireball was fired straight at Corinne.

At the same time, the barrier started to flicker in and out like a broken light-bulb that was about to black out.

"No...no...no, come on! What the heck!" Corinne shook the potato light-bulb, and hit it with her hand.

Then, the barrier dimmed down and went out completely.

Corinne glanced up and the fireball was inches away from her, the potato light-bulb slipped out from her hands. She was frozen in place.

Everything seemed like it was in slow motion, she could see Claire screaming and running towards her with tears streaming down her face.

When she thought that she was toast, she felt a strong grip by the wrist, Corinne glanced down on the hand that grabbed her and saw a familiar gem bangle. By the next second, she found herself being pulled into a warm hug, a pair of strong arms circled around her waist.

A shimmering light glow from the gem bangle as a shield formed in front of them.

Boom!

The collision between the attack and the shield resulted in a huge explosion, Claire who was running towards Corinne almost got blown away.

When the smoke faded away, Corinne opened her eyes and met Quinn's concerned gaze.

"Are you okay?" Quinn asked.

Corinne nodded, then she felt Quinn's weight on her.

"Good, because I just got weak in my knees," Quinn mumbled, "I don't know what got over me when I ran here."

If it weren't for the situation that they were in right now, Corinne would let out a chuckle. She was wondering how the timid Quinn would ran over to save her from becoming toasted Corinne.

"Thanks, Quinn," Corinne said.

"Corinne!" Claire ran up to Corinne, checking her up and down to see if she was okay. Claire took back the light-bulb, and her brows were kneaded.

"I'm so sorry," Claire apologized because of the defected potato light-bulb.

"No worries, I'm fine," Corinne said, "but the dragon wouldn't be!"

Something was coming together, but before Corinne can tidy her thoughts, she needed to keep the dragon busy.

"Hey! You big mutt!" Danny waved his hands in the air, calling for the dragon's attention.

The dragon snarled, flying after Danny.

Mia stood there, trembling with her crystal ball. Sucking in a deep breath, she threw sent her traveler item flying at the dragon.

"Y-you mo-monster! Co-come and get me!" Mia screamed as loud as she could.

The crystal ball flew through the dragon, Mia saw it with her very own eyes, instead of hitting the beast, it flew passed it like it wasn't there.

Mia caught her crystal ball as it got back to her like a boomerang. A yelp escaped her lips when the dragon landed before her in a loud thump.

Gulping in fear, Mia turned as pale as a ghost as she stood there frozen like the statue from the chocolate fountain at the town square.

Thump.

Thump.

Thump.

The sound of the dragon stepping closer to her made Mia's heart beat as fast as a hummingbird. Mia tried to run, but her feet were planted to the ground. She was terrified and couldn't think of what to do.

The dragon stepped closer as she helplessly watched the dragon opened its mouth, revealing its sharp teeth ready to devour her. She tried to scream, but no sound came out.

When Mia thought she was doomed, her hand touched a bump on the edge of her skirt pocket. Quickly, she pulled it out and found that it was the spicy pepper spray her sister had given to Corinne last time. But, Corinne gave it to her instead because she had no use of it.

Lips pursed, Mia pressed on the spray, sending an enormous pepper cloud against the dragon.

At the same time, Danny rummaged through his 'Beginner Big Pack' and pulled out a water gun.

[~~Toy~~ Water Gun-Amusement Park Special Edition (made by Hell Toy Factory, specially designed for Hell Amusement Park 108 Anniversary)

Is it a toy or is it an actual water gun? It may gave you a tiny squirt or an entire river depend on your luck.

Firemen Larry tried to use it to put out a fire during an operation, but he was not heard ever since. Maybe he is retired? Who knows.

Functionality are not guarantee, Hell Toy Factory and Hell Amusement Park will not be responsible for any consequences.

Life is precious, use it at your own risk.]

If Corinne read this, she will definitely scoffed at Hell Travel Agency.

Hell Toy Factory and Hell Amusement Park?

What's this? They are doing a franchise now? Expanding to different industries?

Then, they should really do something about the items they gave out, they were all so unreliable which was true because when Danny used the water gun...

Danny barely skimmed through the description of the gun, "Hey! I've got a water gun and I'm not afraid to use it!"

Danny had this smug look on his face, he was grinning in pure confidence when he aimed the gun at the monster.

Then, a tiny stream came out, it barely touched the dragon and merely left a small puddle on the ground.

Danny: "..."

Mia: "..."

The others: "..."

However, it was enough to pull the dragon's attention.

It stomped over to Danny, growling while Corinne thought: 'Wait! I thought Danny have max luck!'

Danny jumped up with a cry, Mia ran forward with the spicy pepper spray, "Danny, catch!"

As soon as Danny caught it, he sprayed it at the dragon, it was enveloped in the ginormous pepper powder cloud within seconds. The spicy pepper powder was extremely effective at causing temporary paralysis, the dragon was paralyzed.

Corinne grabbed the opening and instantly called out to the beauty in glasses, "Ava!"

When Corinne came face to face with the gigantic fireball earlier, she didn't feel the extreme heat from the flames at all. It was partly the reason why she was startled and stopped in place.

This made Corinne recalled their first day here, when all of their attacks did not worked on the dragon and what Claire told them the other day. Then, when she came face to face with the dragon's fire, something clicked in her mind.

Ava has the truth glasses, which she said so herself that it could break any sort of illusion. She lightly touched her glasses and a screen panel flicked into view in front of her.

A map appeared on the screen, with green dots representing the travelers and a red dot representing the dragon. Ava used both hands to swiftly maneuver the map; she tapped each of the travelers on the map and activated party shared. A second later, futuristic glasses appeared on the faces of all the travelers.

Corinne looked at the dragon and saw that it was really just a small black beast with teeth that looked like they belonged on a T.Rex, it started growling ferociously as it rushed at Corinne with its teeth bared to bite.

In her eyes, under the assistance of the truth glasses; the illusion disappeared, and all that was left was a small black beast charging towards her with its teeth bared to rend her flesh.

Corinne glanced down at the crooked wooden stick in her hand as the mission of this station ran through her mind.

[Mission: Find the lost wand and put the dragon back to hibernation.]

She dashed forward and leapt toward the beast. She lifted up her hand holding the stick and drove it through the heart of the beast.

Put it to sleep?

She's putting the beast to eternal slumber!

With a thud, the beast dropped to the ground, dead; and their glasses faded away along with the illusion.

Silence filled the air as everyone looked at the scene that spread out in front of them, their eyes went from Corinne to the beast that was dead on the ground.

That's it?

The monster is dead just like that?

Corinne was the first one to come back to her senses, she turned around to look at the others.

"Guys, we did it!" Corinne said with a huge grin on her face.

Ding!

[Mission: Find the lost wand and put the dragon back to hibernation.

Status: Completed]

CHAPTER 21

Corinne looked at the screen in front of her. There was a timer counting down toward the moment when she would have to press the confirm button or she could wait for the timer to reach zero and return to the train without pressing anything.

"The-the mission is completed?" Mia said, rubbing her eyes.

"We didn't even find out who the real Eloise was, or seal the dragon," Danny gasped in disbelief.

"Well, the dragon is dead," Quinn said, matter-of-factly.

The mission stated that they needed to retrieve the lost wand and put the dragon to sleep. The information they received mentioned that the dragon was sealed by the royal pâtissier of the kingdom, the wand he used was lost.

The royal pâtissier had an heir, which was Lady Eloise. When they arrived, they found out that there were two Elouises. This was where their minds tricked them.

They thought that the two Elouises were something that the station set up to trick them, making them think that they needed to figure out who the real heir to the royal pâtissier was because they needed the true heir to use the wand and seal the dragon, in order to complete the mission.

This led them into walking two directions, find the wand and also find out who was the real Eloise, when in fact, all they needed to do was to search for the wand and kill the beast themselves.

Speaking of the beast, another thing that deepened their misunderstanding was the dragon.

As soon as they arrived at the Kingdom, they were attacked by a ferocious dragon, it even devoured a traveller right before their eyes.

When they reached the kingdom, they had no idea what was going on which was the reason why the surprise attack of the dragon was so effective on them. It subconsciously gave them the wrong idea that only *Eloise* could seal the dragon.

However, the mission technically did not specify what they should do to make the dragon hibernate.

Claire's eyes went over to Corinne, well... Corinne's method was effective, the dragon was now in eternal slumber.

Ava realized that they made everything complicated because they might have over-analyzed things. After all, this station was merely a trial station for newbie travellers to become a full-fledged travellers.

Actually, if this weren't a trial station, then, finding out who was the real Eloise might have been one of the things they needed to do and they might have needed to uncover more things in this kingdom.

"I think I might know who the real Eloise is," Corinne said, out of the blue.

Everyone turned towards her, waiting for her to continue.

"Neither of them," Corinne stated.

The most obvious clue was they did not recognize the wand at all. Even though, initially, none of them was a hundred percent sure that the stick was the wand. The way the beast was chasing after Corinne, who had the wand, was basically proof that the stick was indeed the royal pâtissier's wand.

However, there were more clues that made Corinne thought that neither of them was the royal pâtissier's daughter.

In the royal pâtissier's diary, he mentioned that he sent his daughter back to his hometown to recuperate from her illness.

Corinne saw the photos of Eloise in the photo album, White Eloise and Black Eloise looked exactly like the Eloise in the photos.

The reason that she thought neither of them was the real Eloise was because White Eloise's purpose was obvious—she wanted to marry the prince. The royal pâtissier had been protecting the kingdom all his life using his magic pastries; in his diary, he mentioned how Eloise had been interested in what he was doing.

So, it was not difficult to guess that in the future, Eloise would follow in his footsteps. However, the way White Eloise had been acting wasn't like Eloise was described by the royal pâtissier in his diary.

As for Black Eloise, Corinne suspected that she was Eloise's lady-in-waiting.

The maid in the picture was Black Eloise. She had grown up with Eloise, who was sent off to the royal pâtissier's hometown because of her illness. With her father's responsibilities, even though he could visit often, she must have still been lonely.

The only one that was her age was her lady-in-waiting, and they grew up together. Their relationship and bond must have been irreplaceable. The only thing that Corinne didn't understand was why she replaced Eloise and pretended to be someone she was not.

When Corinne touched her hand, she noticed Black Eloise's calluses. Eloise was the prince's fiancée and the daughter of the royal pâtissier, she had servants and maids to serve her.

She had everything handed to her, she didn't need to do chores or things on her own. So, why would she have thick calluses? Even if she practiced baking, she wouldn't have such thick calluses.

With all of those findings, Corinne was sure that neither was the real Eloise. The real Eloise must have already died in that shipwreck. That was why, when Corinne went to the attic, Black Eloise was crying, because she lost her friend.

[Ding!

Returning in 5. 4. 3. 2. 1.]

When the countdown ended, Corinne could hear the sound of the train horn and then everything turned black.

[Station: Cakeland Kingdom (Trial Station)

Mission: Find the lost wand and put the dragon back to hibernation.

Status: Complete]

[Reward:

Mission Completion Rank: A +1000 TP

Hidden quest: Uncover the truth behind White Eloise and Black Eloise (50% Completion) +500 TP

Hidden quest: Slay the beast (100% Completion) +1000 TP]

As soon as Corinne got back to the cabin she shared with Claire, this screen flicked out in front of her.

She was stunned when she saw the parts about hidden quests. So, it was true that there was more behind White Eloise and Black Eloise.

Corinne continued to scroll until she saw…

[Titles:

Wild Prankster-You are as childish as a wild child that likes to prank people and enjoy seeing them feeling troubled because of you.

+50 TP

+bear child buff (with this title you will easily attract wild children and get their attention, will you become their underling? Or will you be the one that is reigning over them? 50% chance of increasing or decreasing the affection of wild children)]

Corinne: "…"

Was the system of Hell Express, subtly telling her that she was an unruly kid?

Now she knew why people wanted to get titles. In addition to getting extra TP, you could get buff from the title earned as well.

[Reward Items:

Cakeland Kingdom Medal (Cracked)

-Authority given by the royal prince of Cakeland Kingdom, free access of entry when used. Usage: 1/3

Dragon Slaying Wooden Stick (Stained)

-A wooden stick that was used to slay a baby beast. It was stained by the baby beast's blood.

All monsters will be taunted when the stick is equipped because you were a horrible baby monster killer.

+critical hit buff (5 seconds)

+Taunt]

Corinne: "..."

Okay, so she ended up with a broken medal and a branch that was messed up. She knew Hell Travel Agency and the train was fixed against her. She never got anything that was in tip-top condition.

When Claire saw the title Corinne received, she couldn't hold back a laugh.

"Bear child buff!" Claire laughed, "It suits you so much!"

Corinne narrowed her eyes at her best friend, pouting, "It wasn't that funny. Hmph!"

"Did you get any titles?" Corinne asked.

Claire tapped on a button so both of them could watch the feed.

[Titles:

Resourceful Detective- You can be as stubborn as a mule when you find something, the clue clings to your mind and you won't stop until you get to the bottom to it.

+50 TP

+detective mode (when this mode is turn on, you will have a higher chance of finding clues, at the same time chances of getting into danger also increase. After all, like Detective Canan, everywhere he goes a murder scene follows.]

[Reward Items:

Cakeland Kingdom Chocolate Fountain - You frequented the town square a lot and closely examined it, the kingdom gifts this to you as a souvenir.

The Kingdom is famous for its pastries that can lower the battle instincts of monsters and brought peace to their nation.

When activated there will be a tea party held by the chocolate fountain, attracting the monsters to participate.

Cooldown: 24 hours]

As soon as they finished reading the feed, the sound of a familiar yell and knocking appeared by the door.

"Hell Post! Parcels for King of the World and Doll Queen 1113!"

After they opened their respective packages, Corinne glanced at the miniature chocolate fountain, it was an exact replica from the one they saw at the town square. Then, her eyes turned back to the items she got.

Yup! Hell Express definitely had something against her!

With that thought in mind, Corinne complained to Claire and whined.

Claire looked at her, serious, "Have you ever thought that maybe your luck is just low?"

Corinne gaped, *What?* Corinne felt like she was just struck by lightning, she plopped down on the floor and started to mope. Claire's dolls, except for Jax, all went over and surrounded the mopey Corinne, trying to comfort her.

Claire flipped open her passport and looked at the Cakeland Kingdom stamp on the page.

What they been through flashed through her mind, the time they spent at that station wasn't years, but it felt like an eternity to her; and all of a sudden, she felt like she was in an entirely different world which she *was* and returning home seemed out of reach to her.

She looked out the window and saw only blackness. The windowpane reflected a pale, gray glow back at her, and she could see her reflection on the glass. Confusion and a glint of worry painted her eyes, it was her concern over the unknown they would be facing on this train.

"Claire, Bellina just took the candies I bought from Wilmart! OMG! She ate all of them! Get back here!" Corinne cried.

Claire glanced over and saw Bellina stuff a bunch of candies into her mouth, making her cheeks puff up like a squirrel while running around the room, waving an empty plastic bag in her hand while Corinne ran behind the princess doll.

The other plushies sat by the sideline rooting for either Bellina or Corinne, while Jax looked at the two disapprovingly like they were some misbehaving children.

Claire: "..."

Surprisingly, seeing the ruckus caused by her best friend and her dolls spreading out before her eyes washed away all her worries.

Her eyes went over to the screen of the traveller app and the passport she placed on the table. A smile spread across her flawless features, somehow a sense of security filled her heart. With Corinne and her dolls by her side, she was sure that she could do this!

"Corinne, Bellina!" Claire called out.

Corinne glanced up at her bestie, flashing a beaming smile.

TURN THE PAGE

EPILOGUE

Corinne tapped on the traveller's app and went through all the features in it. After they got back from the Cakeland Kingdom and completed the mission, both she and Claire had become full-fledged travellers.

They finally had full access to the app. The forum was a place for all the travellers to socialize, there was even a tab in the forum for them to add other travellers as friends to engage in private conversation.

When Corinne tapped on the shop, her eyes grew wide.

There were so many things there, some were very odd, like this armor set.

[Magical Rainbow Sparkles Armor Set - Have you ever dreamed of being a magical girl? Look no further! This armor set will make your dream a reality.

Raise the wand that comes with the armor and say the following line to transform: "Friendship is magic! Your magical rainbow sparkles girl/boy is here!"

+friendship buff

+attack buff

+defend buff]

Corinne had to peer her eyes and read it twice just to make sure that she didn't read it wrong.

At the bottom of the description where the price was, she saw: ~~99999~~ 9999 (One day sale! Get it now, it is a steal!)

Corinne: "..."

Who would get this magical girl/boy armor set anyway?

Somewhere on another Hell Express someone pulled out a frilly magical boy outfit that was covered in blinding rainbow glitters.

"Hey, Ben! Look at this cool armor I got! Awesome right?"

Ben: "!"

Ben: "What the heck! Why do you waste your TP like this, John?!"

Back at Hell Express Six, Corinne looked at the Magical Rainbow Sparkles Armor Set, it had this huge red 'Sold Out' sticker plastered over the page.

Feeling disbelief, she turned to Claire, wanting to tell her about this when she saw Claire aggressively typing on her cellphone.

"What are you doing?" Corinne asked.

Bzzz

"Attention all Hell Express Six travellers, we will be stopping at Willowdale Town for the next station…"

Hearing that, both Corinne and Claire exchanged a glance.

ACKNOWLEDGMENTS

I wanted to thank my family and my best friend for being so supportive.

I will have to admit that throughout the entire process of writing this book, there were a lot of self-doubts that make me this close to shelf this book and not let it see the light. It was my sisters and my bestie that push me through, it was their encouragement that make me finish the story of Corinne and Claire. It was thanks to them that Corinne and Claire had their adventure.

Thanks, Amelie for listening to my rambles on the ideas that I have for this story and the conversations I have with you always led to inspirations, thanks Claire for always encouraging me when I wanted to give up.

Chrisandra, you're a lifesaver and an amazing editor; I am so happy that I found you and was able to work with you on this project.

And, to you, my reader; thank you for giving my story a chance! If you like it, don't forget to leave a review, even if it is just a short sentence it will also mean the world to me!

ABOUT AUTHOR

Hell Express is Cherilyn Yap's debut series. Cherilyn loves reading, writing and anime, which is explored in this gamelit adventure. Those who enjoyed the *Hunger Games* and the popular Netflix show *Squid Games* will love this epic ride.

CONNECT WITH CHERILYN ON:

https://linktr.ee/cherilynyap